"Why did you do that, Elam?" Naomi's voice was a low growl.

"Do what?"

"Volunteer us to organize the auction." Color rose in her cheeks. "I have a sick *bobbeli* to care for. When am I supposed to work on this? And with you, of all people."

Her anger pierced him. When had their love turned to such bitterness?

"I thought you'd want to be part of it."

"I have no desire to do anything with you."

"Simon and Sylvia are counting on us." *Ja*, it would be difficult to see her on a regular basis, but maybe they would discover a path beyond the hurt.

"I suggest you volunteer someone else. It won't be me." She turned to leave.

He caught her by the elbow. "Won't you reconsider?"

"Leave me alone, Elam. Because of what you did to my brother, you're the last person in the world I would ever organize an auction with." She yanked free of his grasp.

This time, he let her go.

That one mistake, that one accident. Could she ever pardon the man she had once loved?

Bestselling author **Liz Tolsma** loves to write so much it's often hard to tear her away from her computer. When she closes her laptop's lid, she might walk her hyperactive Jack Russell terrier, weed her large perennial garden or binge on HGTV shows. She's married to her high school sweetheart, and together they adopted three children. She's proud to be the mom of a US marine.

Books by Liz Tolsma

Love Inspired

The Amish Widow's New Love

The Amish Widow's New Love

Liz Tolsma

HARLEQUIN® LOVE INSPIRED®

Recycling programs
for this product may
not exist in your area.

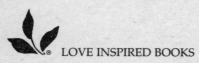

LOVE INSPIRED BOOKS

ISBN-13: 978-1-335-42805-9

The Amish Widow's New Love

Copyright © 2018 by Christine Cain

www.Harlequin.com

Printed in U.S.A.

I, even I, am he that blotteth out
thy transgressions for mine own sake,
and will not remember thy sins.
—*Isaiah* 43:25

To my sisters, Carolyn and Elaine.
Thank you for all the love, support and
fun throughout the years. I'm privileged to have
gotten to be your big sister. Love you guys!

Acknowledgments

Special thanks to Richard Dawley
of Amish Insight and Judy Cook from
The Woodshed Amish Tours in Augusta,
Wisconsin, for your help and knowledge
about the Amish in Wisconsin. I so
appreciate everything you taught me!

Chapter One

Naomi Miller crossed the Masts' side yard between the house and the barn, her brother Aaron beside her, bumping over the ground in his motorized wheelchair, the smell of new-cut grass assailing her. The shouts of the young people playing volleyball engulfed her as they cheered for each spike and every point gained. Near the metal shed, a group of teenage girls huddled together, white prayer *kapp*-covered heads bent together. Bunches of laughing boys hugged the barn's back wall.

Her stomach knotted. Years had passed since she'd been to a singing. She didn't belong here. This was all for her brother. That's the one reason she came. He should be a part of the gathering.

Aaron tightened his shoulders and twisted

in his chair, his broad-brimmed straw hat askew. "I shouldn't be here."

"Nonsense. We made a deal. If I came, you would, too."

"But they'll look at me funny." He pounded on his unfeeling, useless legs.

"People here are used to the chair. And at least you're single and have no children. How does it look for me, a widow with an infant son, to be at a singing?" Wait, did she hear Joseph crying? *Nein.* She shook her head. Her son remained at home with Mamm, safe and sound asleep.

"At least you—"

"Enough of that. We'll both have a *wunderbaar* time." She swallowed hard. Maybe it wouldn't turn out to be a lie. But her gut clenched when a picture of Joseph flashed through her mind. She wiped her sweaty palms down her dark purple dress. What if Mamm couldn't get him to eat enough? What if he had trouble breathing again? Maybe Aaron was right. Maybe this was a bad idea.

He lifted his hat from his head and mussed his blond curls. "No girl is going to want a man in a wheelchair. That's why I haven't been to a singing since the accident. I wish you would never have suggested this to Mamm and Daed."

She did, too. But what was done was done. "Which young lady do you have your eye on?" If she concentrated on Aaron, she might get through this night.

He turned to her. "Can we please go home?"

"Out of the question. Mamm and Daed would be disappointed if we didn't stay for at least a little while. So if you don't tell me who you're going to sit next to, I'll pick out the prettiest girl and bring her to you."

All the color drained from his face until it matched the color of Mamm's bleached sheets. "You wouldn't."

"Don't make me show you I'm serious." She couldn't quite force a smile to her lips.

"Hold on. You don't want to be here either."

He'd always been too perceptive. "What makes you think that?"

"When you used to come to singings, your face would light up. You loved these gatherings. I don't see that in your eyes now."

"It's not the same." Not since… *Nein*, she couldn't think about all the terrible losses. But Aaron had given her an out. "Fine, we can leave. I'll get the buggy and be back in a moment."

"*Nein*, I'll get it. I don't like the way you drive. Much too slow for me." Daed had modified Aaron's buggy with a ramp so he could roll in and out. He liked to spur his horse to trot as fast as possible. "You can stay. I think Solomon Mast wants to drive you home."

"He may want to, but he's not going to. I'm not interested in him. Or in anyone for that matter. It's only been a year since Daniel died." When she spun around to go to the buggy, she hit something. Someone. Hard.

The masculine scent of wood and horses enveloped her. The man grabbed her upper arm and prevented her from falling. The warmth of his hand seeped through her dress's cotton sleeve. "Be careful." His deep voice resonated in her ears.

She stared into eyes the same green as the spring grass beneath her feet. For a moment, she forgot to breathe, the wind knocked out of her. Then she drew in a gulp of air and stepped back. "I'm sorry. I wasn't watching where I was going."

"Are you alright?"

She nodded, and lost her breath again. She knew those eyes. Much too well. Naomi's heart throbbed in her chest as she took in the man's straight reddish hair and his ruddy cheeks. "Elam Yoder. What are you doing here?"

"Hello to you, too." His words were strained.

He wore Amish clothes. Dark pants, a light blue shirt and a straw hat.

"You've come back?" She worked to keep her voice as controlled and distant as possible, even as she trembled from head to toe. How dare he show his face in this district again.

"I have."

"Why?"

"Because of Daed's stroke. He needs my help around the farm until Isaac can sell his ranch in Montana and get home. So I'm here."

Aaron piped up behind her. "Hello, Elam."

"Aaron. It's good to see you. How are you?"

"Just on my way home. This isn't for me." He nodded in the barn's direction where a clutch of young women giggled at what the young men said.

Elam shuffled his feet. Seeing Aaron must make him uncomfortable. All the better. He should be uneasy. Should be ashamed of himself.

"I'll go to the barn with you, if you'd like." Elam took a step in Aaron's direction.

Naomi jumped in between them. "That won't be necessary. This wasn't a *gut* idea for either one of us. We'll be going now."

In the distance, footsteps crunched on the gravel driveway. Not some latecomer strolling up the road. Quick, light steps. Running.

In the fading daylight, she made out the shape and size of the figure. Her younger brother, Samuel.

He slid to a halt in front of them, panting, sweat dotting his brow. "Mamm sent me for you. Joseph woke up and is fussing, and she thinks he's running a fever. His breathing is raspy."

A cry rose from her chest, but she trapped it in her throat. "Is he okay?"

"I don't know. Mamm just wanted me to get you. She didn't say anything else, but I think you should hurry."

Her entire body turned cold. "Let's go." For her son's sake, they had to be fast. "Aaron, get the buggy. Joseph's labored breathing isn't *gut*. The doctor told me to bring him right in with any kind of respiratory problem."

Before she could move, Elam grabbed her. Oh, the temptation to sink into his arms for comfort. Instead, she squirmed in his grip. "My *bobbeli* is sick. I have to get home to him."

Elam held on to her. "I still have my truck. I fixed it, and my license hasn't expired. Let me take you home."

If possible, her heart rate elevated. "You want me to put my life in your hands?"

"It will be faster."

She'd heard the crash that night, right in front of their house. She couldn't wipe the sound of crunching metal out of her mind. Aaron's screams. "I can't. I can't trust you. I will never trust you again."

Naomi's voice was as icy as the pond in January. Elam shivered. Both at her words and the sight of Aaron in his wheelchair. The young man worked the controls on the chair, spinning around until the wheel caught on a rock. He was stuck.

Stuck in the wheelchair Elam had condemned him to. Every muscle in his body clenched. After three years, the vivid images hadn't faded. Neither had the tinkling of shattered glass. Nor the echoes of Aaron's cries of agony.

He had stripped this man of his vitality and relegated him to a life of struggles and pain.

"Come, Naomi, Joseph needs you." Her brother Samuel tugged at her arm.

Elam shook his head. He'd heard Naomi had married Daniel Miller. What, then, was she doing at a singing meant for singles?

Naomi snapped to attention. She massaged the end of the string of her prayer *kapp*.

"We could get to the clinic faster in the truck. I know I was rebellious when I was young, buying a truck and a cell phone when I was thinking about leaving the Amish. Only you held me here. That and the fact they couldn't kick me out because I hadn't been baptized. But I don't have my cell phone anymore, so I won't be distracted. You can trust me. The truck is in our barn across the street. In a few minutes, we can be on our way."

They didn't have Rumspringa here like back East, but Elam had come close to it. "Sam, go home with Aaron. I'll go with you, Elam, on one condition. You have to drive slowly. But get me to Joseph as fast as possible."

Elam gave a two-beat laugh. "I'll try and do the impossible." Not giving her time to change her mind, he sprinted down the gravel driveway and across the street to his daed's farm. He flung open the barn door, his footsteps reverberating in the silence as he went to his truck.

In the Englisch world, he had needed it to get around. He slipped inside and retrieved the key from under the floor mat. As he slid the key into the ignition and turned it, he drew in a deep breath, his heart pounding. He had thought his truck-driving days were behind him. The engine roared to life.

He shifted into Drive, stepped on the gas and pulled from the barn. Naomi hadn't changed. Big, almost purple-blue eyes in a heart-shaped face. A delicate nose. How she tugged on her *kapp* string when she was nervous.

His breath stuck in his throat. She had turned her back on him after the accident. They had been planning their wedding, but she refused to listen to his apologies. Refused to hear him out. And less than a year later, she had married someone else.

And where was Daniel? Shouldn't he have been with her? Or watching their son?

As his headlights swept the road in front of him, they illuminated Naomi, who stood at the end of the drive. He stopped in front of her, and she climbed into the backseat.

"You can sit up front." He adjusted his rearview mirror.

She buckled her belt. "This is where I always sit in a car." Like she would do with any *Englisch* driver. That's what she treated him as. An outsider.

"Where do you live?"

"At my parents' house." She gripped the edge of the seat.

Had they retired to the *dawdi haus* already?

They weren't old and still had young children. Wouldn't Daniel have his own place? Nothing about Naomi made sense. "So, how old is your *bobbeli*?"

"Three months."

"Daniel must be worried if he sent for you."

The roar of silence filled the truck cab.

"Naomi? Did you hear me?"

"My husband died almost a year ago."

Elam blew out his breath. How awful for her. "I'm sorry. I didn't know."

They passed a few farms, bright white light spilling from the windows of fancy Englisch homes. Softer, paler light flickered from the plain white Amish houses. He glanced over his shoulder. "That must have been hard."

Naomi swiped away a stray tear. "It was. He fell from a roof. But Joseph was a wonderful surprise. His coming eased some of the hurt. I'll have a piece of Daniel with me forever."

He returned his attention to the road. Daniel always had his eye on her. Elam shouldn't be surprised she'd married him. Unable to forgive Elam for his one mistake, she had moved on with her life. Had turned her back on what they shared and became another man's wife. The pain that pierced his chest startled him. That part of his life should have been far behind him.

He shook his head. Such thoughts were useless.

He didn't have time to dwell on this information as they soon arrived at her parents' home and her father's woodworking shop, where he had once worked. Before he could come around to help her out, she unlatched the belt, slid from the truck, and slammed the door shut. He jogged behind her to the house, the *bobbeli's* weak, raspy cries reaching them as they crossed the front porch.

A moment after entering through the kitchen and into the living room, Naomi was at her mother's side. Sarah Bontrager rocked the infant in a well-worn rocking chair, and Naomi's sister Laura was at their mamm's side. Joseph coughed, deep and tight, the sound tugging at Elam.

Sarah wiped the *bobbeli's* perspiration-dotted brow. "You got here fast. That's *gut*. He was fussy, so I picked him out of his cradle. The heat of his body radiated through his clothes. When he hacked, such a terrible cough, I sent Sam for you right away. I can't get him to eat either."

Naomi felt her son's forehead and widened

her eyes. "We need to get him to urgent care. Now. With his heart condition…"

Sarah cradled Joseph. "Laura, tell Daed to run and call Frank Jameson and see if he can drive. Naomi and I will get Joseph ready."

Elam stepped from the shadows. "No need. My truck's right outside, warmed and ready to go."

Both women stared at him with open mouths, as if he'd appeared out of thin air.

Sarah stood from the rocker, handed the *bobbeli* to Naomi and then clenched her hands. "Elam Yoder. You still have that truck?"

That truck. The one that had caused so much damage. They would never let him forget. Not this family. Not this district. He stepped back. "*Ja*, I do. I brought Naomi from the singing. I can take her."

"No need." Naomi shook her head so hard it was surprising it didn't fly off her shoulders.

And her mind was made up.

She hustled by him into the kitchen, and he followed. From a peg by the back door, she grabbed a diaper bag. "Frank Jameson can be here in less than fifteen minutes. There's no reason for you to make the trip. The doctor might send us to Madison."

She was that afraid of him? Would his actions from that night haunt him forever?

The little one coughed. "We're wasting time debating this. If you go with me, I can have you there fifteen minutes sooner than Frank."

Naomi's daed entered the kitchen from the hall. "I'll go phone for Frank."

Elam suppressed a sigh. "If the *bobbeli* is so sick, you shouldn't waste time."

"And let my daughter and grandson end up like my son?" Leroy Bontrager crossed his arms, jaw tight.

Naomi's hand trembled as she brushed her boy's cheek. "He's so warm."

Joseph gasped and coughed.

"Let me take you. Please. I can help. I want to."

She glanced away from him, then back in his direction. "I don't know."

"Naomi."

She gritted her teeth. "Fine. I'll get Joseph's blanket, and we can leave. Mamm, you'll come with me, right?"

"Of course." Sarah entered the kitchen, her sweater already in her hands.

Leroy stepped to within inches of Elam. "If anything happens to any of them, I will hold you responsible. You be careful with that truck. They are precious cargo. This is only because the need is so urgent."

Naomi placed the *bobbeli* into the car seat on the hall floor. His face. Wide-set eyes, thick lips and a flat nose, all positioned in a round face. His Englisch boss at the construction company had a daughter like that. He called it Down syndrome. What a burden for Naomi to carry, on top of losing her husband.

The object of his thoughts tucked a fuzzy blue blanket around Joseph then swept up the car seat by the handle. "We're ready. Let's go. Do you know the way?"

"*Ja.* Don't worry. We'll be there soon."

"It can't be soon enough." A tear trickled down Naomi's cheek.

Elam held himself back from wiping it away. She wouldn't allow him to comfort her.

Sarah rubbed her daughter's back. "We must trust God to do what is right."

Elam held the door open for the two women. As he turned to shut it, he caught sight of Leroy, who glared at him.

Elam shivered and then stepped into the chilly Wisconsin night.

Chapter Two

Naomi stroked her son's hot, damp cheek with one hand and clung to the edge of the truck's back seat with the other as they raced toward the clinic. Joseph cried weak, pitiful mews, stopping only to catch his breath, which he did far too often. Her throat burned. "Can't you go faster, Elam?"

"I'm speeding as it is. We're in town. Not far now."

The trip had taken much too long. Why did the clinic have to be so far? The dim glow of the streetlights illuminated Joseph's red face.

Mamm reached over the car seat and patted Naomi's hand. "Don't worry so. We'll be there soon. You just drive careful now, Elam."

He clung to the steering wheel and peered out the windshield. At least he heeded Mamm's instructions.

After another eternity, they pulled into the parking lot. Elam rolled to a stop as she grabbed Joseph's car seat and hopped out, Mamm sliding out the other side.

"I'll park and be right—"

Naomi slammed the door.

By the time she carried her wailing child inside and registered him at the desk, Elam had joined them. Why had he come? Better for him to stay in that truck. Mamm was here.

The waiting room buzzed with activity. Sick children. Some virus or bug must be going around. Maybe Joseph had picked up his illness from one of the children at the church service two weeks ago. Mamm calmly sat on one of the chairs on the far side of the room. Probably praying.

Elam sat across from her, clasping his straw hat with his big, work-roughened hands. She paced the room and jiggled Joseph on her hip. Elam patted the chair on his left. "Come sit, Naomi. You're going to wear yourself out."

"I can't. What's taking them so long?"

"Fretting about it won't make them call you sooner. Now sit. I can hold Joseph if you want a break."

"Nein, denki." The harsh words flew from her lips, but she would not give her son to him. Never. "I'm sorry, Elam. I shouldn't

have been short just now. I am thankful for your help tonight."

She moved the car seat from the chair beside Mamm and sat. Joseph's little body melded into hers. She kissed his burning cheek.

Elam peered at Joseph. "Does he often get sick?"

"The doctor said if he got a respiratory infection, it could be very bad. He has a hole in his heart, and that is not good for his lungs. I don't fully understand, and it's hard to explain. It's dangerous for him to be sick." Like always, he managed to get her to open up. To share her heart. She couldn't allow that. He'd broken it once before. She wouldn't give him a chance to do it again. She pursed her lips together.

A nurse dressed in bright blue scrubs emerged from the doorway to the side of the desk. "Joseph Miller?"

Naomi gathered Joseph's diaper bag and stood. She and Mamm followed the nurse into one of the small rooms and sat in the chairs beside the little desk.

Naomi leaned over, willing her hands to stop shaking.

Julie, as the nurse had introduced herself, took Joseph's history, his blood pressure, his temperature and his pulse, and typed everything into the computer. "So he hasn't been sick that long?"

"A sniffle or two this morning, but I didn't think anything of it. I put him in bed before I went out. My mamm was watching him, and she sent for me not too long afterward to tell me he was crying and wouldn't eat." She shouldn't have left him. It was her fault he got so sick. Mamm pulled her into a side hug.

"Any tugging on the ears?"

"Not that I've noticed." Naomi forced the words around the lump in her throat.

Mamm patted her hand.

"Cough?"

"Yes, deep and tight."

The questions went on. Mamm sat beside her until Julie finished. "The doctor will be in soon. If you need anything, just holler. I'll be right down the hall."

As the nurse closed the door, Naomi worried the hem of her sleeve. Mamm rubbed her shoulder. "He'll be fine. He's made of sturdy stuff."

"I'm scared." Her insides quivered.

"I know. But God is watching out for him."

"I could lose him." More tears streamed down her face.

"I know, my daughter, I know. But the doctors will take *gut* care of him. He will be fine. You'll see."

Mamm's words washed over her, but her stomach still tightened. "Even with Aaron's accident and Daniel's fall, I never felt like this. So helpless. So frightened of being alone." She nestled Joseph against her, the one good thing in her life.

Dear God, don't take him from me. I can't stand to lose him.

Naomi kissed her sleeping son on his cool cheek and pulled up the blanket to his chin, careful not to rock the cradle and wake him. Now, with several doses of antibiotics in him, his breathing was once again normal. Such a scare he'd given her the other day. *Denki, Lord, that he's well.*

As well as he could be for a child with a hole in his heart.

He puckered his blue lips and puckered his mouth in his sleep. With one more kiss, Naomi slipped out the bedroom door.

Mamm, a basket of laundry in her hands, met her at the bottom of the steps. "Ready for your first day back at the bakery?"

Naomi's stomach churned. Other than the singing on Sunday, she hadn't been away from Joseph since his birth. And look how that had turned out. "I don't want to leave him. What if he needs me? He did when I went to the singing."

"Laura and I will be here all day. You'll be across the street. His getting sick had nothing to do with you leaving him. It's *gut* for you to get out of the house, even if only for a few hours of the day. If you don't, you'll go stir-crazy in no time. And a happy mamm makes for a happy *bobbeli*."

"Still…"

"Off with you. Take your mind from your worries for a while. Go, before I make you iron all of this."

Naomi tried to smile at Mamm's joke. Ironing was the worst form of torture. "I'm going, I'm going. Anything to avoid that." She gave a slight chuckle. "But you get me if Joseph needs me for anything at all. Anything."

"I will." Mamm kissed her on the cheek in much the same way she had kissed Joseph. Her tight muscles relaxed a little bit.

Before she knew it, Naomi stood on the threshold of the walkout basement's back door leading to the downstairs bakery. After drawing in a deep breath, she stepped inside, warmth enveloping her, the yeasty aroma of bread, doughnuts and cinnamon rolls welcoming her.

She hadn't been here as an employee since Joseph's birth. The people, the routine, the work had brought her a measure of comfort after Daniel's death. Perhaps Mamm was right. Maybe being here would keep her from worrying about her son, even if only for a few hours.

Rachel Miller, her sister-in-law and best friend, scurried into the hall. "Naomi, welcome back. How *gut* it is to see you." She wrapped her in a hug. "How is Joseph doing?"

"Fine now. But that illness was one of the scariest things that I've ever had to experience." Joseph was her precious only child. His sickness could have been serious, even life-threatening.

"The Lord is gracious. And it is *gut* to have you beside me again, even if it's only a few days a week."

They entered the kitchen, and Naomi stared at the stoves lining the walls, the big sink in the back and the large metal table in the middle where the women did most of their work. Rachel squeezed her shoulder. "Are you okay? You sure you're up for this?"

She had to be. "*Ja*, except it's almost like I'm dreaming. But Mamm says it's *gut* for me to get out of the house for a while, and the money will help with the repairs to the *dawdi haus* so I can move in there. Have a measure of independence."

"Whatever the reason you came back to work, I'm glad you're here."

They set to their tasks, Rachel kneading dough that would become pretzels, and Naomi kneading seven-grain bread. Before long, the rhythm of the work settled her.

"You crazy old man, what are you doing?" A voice carried from the back room.

Naomi turned to Rachel. "Is that Sylvia Herschberger?"

"Sounds like it."

"Just getting this flour you wanted."

Naomi chuckled. "*Ja*, that's Simon answering her."

"Let me help you with that."

Elam? Was that his voice? Her stomach fluttered in her midsection. Which was ridiculous. He had helped them when Joseph got sick, but that was all.

"Watch out."

Boom. Crash. Bang.

"Simon!" Sylvia screeched.

Naomi wiped her hands on her apron and scurried to the back room. "*Ach*, Simon, oh no."

The older man lay on the floor, his right leg jutting out at an odd angle. Elam pulled a ladder off him. Sylvia stood over her husband, wringing her hands. Flour covered all three of them and the floor. Dust floated on the sunlit air.

Naomi hurried to his side. "What can I do? Tell me how to help."

Elam's green eyes widened when he saw her. "We'll need an ambulance."

Rachel reached Naomi. "I'll run down the street to call for one."

Naomi knelt beside the gray-haired man, his hat crushed underneath him. "Simon?"

"Oh, my leg." He spoke the words through gritted teeth.

"I told you not to climb up there for the flour." His wife paced the room stacked with large quantities of baking supplies, her black shoes leaving prints on the dusty floor. "Why didn't you wait for Elam to get here to do it?"

Elam motioned for Sylvia to stop. "That doesn't matter. Right now, let's get him comfortable while we wait for the ambulance."

Sylvia wiped a tear from the corner of her eye. "There are pillows and a blanket on our bed upstairs." She wobbled on her feet.

"I'll get them. And you look like you need a chair." Naomi held her by the arm. "Lean against the wall. Will you be okay while I grab a seat for you?"

Sylvia nodded.

Elam placed the ladder against the shelves. "I'll help you carry everything."

Naomi opened her mouth to object, but shut it right away. Instead, she followed him up the stairs. "Why are you here?"

"I could ask you the same question." He opened the door to the family's living quarters.

"I'm trying to scrape together some money to repair the *dawdi haus* for myself and my son."

"And Simon asked me to make a few new picnic tables for the Englisch to sit on when the weather's nice. The ones they have now are unsteady and falling apart. They're giving me a chance to prove myself and show people I'm serious about returning. I'm hoping it will lead to a new business venture. How is Joseph, by the way?"

She popped into the Herschbergers' bedroom and pulled a couple of pillows and a red-and-blue wedding-ring quilt from the bed before returning to the kitchen, where Elam grabbed a chair. "Fine. And once more, *denki* for what you did for us when he got sick."

"I'm happy I was at the singing to give you a ride." His smile was tight, like he forced it.

They descended the stairs and returned

to the Herschbergers. Naomi knelt beside
Simon. "Here you are." She lifted him enough
to slide two pillows under his head, and then
covered him with the quilt. Elam helped Sylvia into the chair.

Simon grasped the coverlet, his knuckles
turning white. "Guess I'm going to have to
go to the hospital."

Naomi took care not to hurt him when she
straightened the quilt over his twisted knee.
"You've broken your leg. And done a good
job of it. Let's hope that's all."

"How long do you think I will be out of
commission?" Simon groaned.

"Only a doctor can answer that." What was
taking that ambulance so long?

A furrow appeared on Simon's brow. "But
the auction is coming up."

All the air rushed from Naomi's lungs.
That auction was to raise money for medical
needs in the district. Like for Joseph's surgery. And Aaron's ongoing expenses. Simon
did most of the organizing. How would they
pay for anything without the funds the event
raised?

Elam peered out the door. "I hear the siren.
The ambulance must be just down the road.
You hang on."

Simon winced as he nodded. "And you and Naomi will take over coordinating the auction."

"You want us to do it?" Elam spun around to face inside.

"You'll do a fine job. I won't have to worry with the two of you in charge."

Elam hawed for a moment. "I'm not sure."

"Make an old man happy. Let me rest well."

Simon couldn't be serious. "*Nein*, we can't." They couldn't.

"She's right. It would be too—"

"Nonsense. You can make it work."

Elam shifted his weight from one foot to the other. "Fine, we'll do it."

A bolt of lightning couldn't have shocked her more. "We will?"

Chapter Three

The sirens wailed as the ambulance raced from the bakery's parking lot, carrying Simon Herschberger to the hospital, his wife at his side. Elam relaxed his shoulders. His friend and mentor was in *gut* hands now.

He turned to walk up the driveway, back to his wagon loaded with lumber for the picnic tables. The crowd of curious Englischers dispersed, some to their cars, others into the line for their baked goods.

Naomi scurried in front of him, blocking his path, her hands on her hips. "What did you do that for?" Her voice was a low growl.

"Do what?" His innocence was an act, one she was sure to see through.

"Volunteer us, me, to organize the auction. How could you do that without consulting me? Do you know how much time and effort that takes?" Color rose in her cheeks. "And I have a very sick *bobbeli* to care for. One who needs surgery as soon as possible. When am I supposed to have the time to work on this with you? *You*, of all people."

The shine in her face got his blood to pumping. Her anger pierced him. When had their love turned to such bitterness? He peered around. Several of the Englisch stared at them. "You might want to keep your voice down." He nodded in the direction of the bakery.

She whipped around and then turned to face him, the red that had graced her cheeks dissipating.

"That's why I said you and I would put it together. Much of the money raised will go to pay Joseph's medical bills and my daed's. You're as invested in this as I am. I thought you'd want to be part of it."

"I have no desire to do anything other than sew a few quilts and bake a couple of pies. Besides that, leave me out of it."

"Simon and Sylvia are counting on us." *Ja*, it would be difficult to see her on a regular basis, but he could find a way to do it. Couldn't she? Maybe they would be able to discover a path beyond the hurt.

"I suggest you volunteer someone else. It

won't be me." She turned her back to him once more and started for the bakery.

He caught her by the elbow. Why he did it when she had just lashed out at him, he couldn't say. "Won't you reconsider?"

"Who's making a scene now?"

He bent to her height and whispered in her ear, the clean scent of soap tickling his nose. "Please assist me. I'll do most of the work."

"Aren't you helping your daed on the farm? Since his stroke, I think he'd need you." She kept her gaze forward.

"I am, but Isaac will soon be back to take over the day-to-day operations. You know farming isn't my life's calling."

"Go build your picnic tables, Elam, and leave me alone." She yanked free of his grasp and scuttled to the kitchen.

This time, he let her go.

He scrubbed his face. Would he ever live down what he'd done years ago? It had been an accident, and she had turned her back on him when everyone else did. Then and now it seemed she couldn't pardon the man she had claimed to love. He lost himself in the work in front of him, sawing and screwing and sanding until he shed his jacket and wiped sweat from his forehead, the day warm for early spring.

The line of customers stretched out the door, around the path, up the steps and into the parking lot. Naomi and the others inside would be busy. But he glanced up as a group of Amish women exited through the back door. And there Naomi was, in the middle of the bunch, a slight smile touching her lips as she reacted to whatever Rachel said.

He averted his gaze. Bumping into her so much made being back in the district more difficult. Part of him still loved her as much as when he left. But another part of him ached at her hard-heartedness. Motherhood added a soft roundness to her face, color to her cheeks, straightness to her back. Though he had first thought she hadn't changed, she was not the woman he left behind.

"What are you doing there?"

Elam sucked in a breath. Rachel peered over his shoulder as he screwed two pieces of wood together. "You want to scare a man to death?"

"*Ach*, it's not that easy to frighten you. If I had really wanted to, I would have snuck up even quieter." Rachel stood with her arms crossed.

"So you were trying to give me a heart attack. Isn't it enough we've had an ambulance here once already today?"

Naomi tugged on Rachel's arm. "Come on, let's have some lunch. The other girls are already sitting down to eat. It's busy, and they'll need us back soon. Especially with Sylvia not here."

Rachel nodded at Elam. "Why don't you join us?"

"*Ja*, I need a break." Elam wiped his hands on his pants. "Let me wash up, and I'll join you."

A scowl appeared on Naomi's face. Well, she may not be happy about it, but that wouldn't stop him from getting a bite to eat. More than anything, he wanted her forgiveness. Everyone's forgiveness.

After a stop in the washroom to scrub his hands and face, he joined the girls at a table away from where the customers ate their baked goods. Still the crowds stared, giggled and even pointed.

The only spot available was on the end of the bench, right beside Naomi. He plopped down, and she scooted as far away from him as possible, knocking elbows with Rachel as she unwrapped her sandwich from the wax paper. Rachel scraped some dilly chicken salad onto a paper plate and handed it to Elam.

He ate a few bites before turning to Naomi.

"When would be a *gut* time to get together to work on the auction? I can speak to Sylvia when she returns from the hospital, find out what Simon has planned and what we still need to do. Maybe tomorrow night?"

"I told you I'm not working with you. You volunteered for this. Take care of it on your own." Her words were so icy, her breath should have puffed in small clouds in front of her.

"Wait." He grabbed her by the forearm. She winced and pulled away. Should he press the matter? *Ja*, what did he have to lose? He had promised Simon. "You haven't heard the best part yet."

"There's more?" She hugged herself.

"We can make it the biggest, most successful auction yet if you tell your story about Daniel and Joseph to the newspapers across the state. The Englisch will flock here to buy quilts and furniture and baked goods, all to support a widow and her little son."

She clenched her fists and sat back, almost tilting off the bench. "You want me to do what?" She almost screeched by the end.

He closed his eyes and grimaced. Once again, he had managed to anger her. He couldn't seem to do anything else.

* * *

A cold sweat broke out all over Naomi. "Absolutely not." She kept her voice low to avoid drawing attention from the bakery's customers for the second time today but stern enough for Elam to be clear about her desires. "I will not help you with the auction. And I will not, under any circumstance, go to the papers." She wadded up her sandwich wrapper and stuffed it into her bag.

He opened his eyes, and a vein in his neck throbbed. "After all this time, are you still so angry?"

Her thoughts scrambled in her brain like eggs in a frying pan. How did she identify this burning in her chest? Anger? Or something just the opposite? "So much has changed since the night of the accident. So much that can never be undone. Don't you understand?"

"I do. But you once claimed to love me. Didn't that mean anything? Can't you forgive me?"

She breathed in and out, the back of her neck aching. "You ask too many difficult questions. Ones I don't have the answers for, that I may never have the answers for. I'm dealing with my husband's loss and my son's serious illness and disability. Isn't that enough?"

The other women gathered the remains of their lunches and meandered inside to resume work. Naomi rose, as well. With a brush of his hand against hers, time stood still. Just like years ago, her knees went mushy, and she thumped into her seat. She nodded at Rachel to stay. Her friend shrugged and bit into a peanut butter cookie.

Elam plowed ahead. "The auction is just a couple weeks away. If you're going to tell your story to the papers, we have to contact the reporters soon. You want to give their readers enough notice so they can make plans to come here."

"It's bad enough to have these people here, staring at us. We're nothing more than a tourist attraction." She motioned wide, her gesture sweeping over the lot packed with cars, one pulling up the gravel driveway every couple of minutes. "But to encourage even more of them to come, that's not a *gut* idea."

"What are they going to do?"

"Disrupt our lives. Mine has been stretched and changed until I don't recognize it. I don't need any further interference." Couldn't he go away and leave her alone? Just leave her in peace? "Why are you even back in the area? Do you want to bring the Englisch to us?"

"*Nein*, not at all."

But he had abandoned her. When she'd gone to him for comfort, he had left. And hadn't returned until now. "Don't you miss the friends you made out there?"

"I missed the Amish much more."

"And your family? How do they feel about you being back? Won't they miss you when you leave again?"

"I'm home to stay, Naomi."

She couldn't help but be doubtful. *Forever* didn't mean much to him.

He stabbed his plastic fork on his plate. "Listen to me. The most important person to you in your life is your son, *nein*?"

"*Ja*, that's right."

"He's beautiful, Naomi. Such a gift from the Lord. All you have left of Daniel."

Rachel stared straight ahead, her eyes filling with tears. "My brother would have done anything for his little boy."

"He would have been a *wunderbaar* daed." Naomi patted Rachel's hand.

Elam nodded. "Parents are like that. They would make any sacrifice for their children. Even though I'm not a daed yet, I know I would walk to the moon if I thought it would help my children. Isn't giving Joseph the best chance at a happy, healthy life worth anything you might have to do to make that happen?"

Tears now clouded Naomi's eyes. The way Elam had of putting things... "Of course. That's why I'm working here. That's why I take him to the doctor, why I walk the floor with him at night, sing to him, love him. But there are things I can think of that I wouldn't do."

"Wouldn't you do anything that was legal, moral and ethical?"

"Maybe." Every time Elam came near her, she couldn't think straight. He spoke with pretty words and was very convincing. If he were Englisch, perhaps he would be a lawyer.

"All you would have to do is sit down with a couple of reporters and tell your story. Tell them how much you love Joseph. What he means to you. And the good the auction does, not only for your son, but for people like Aaron and Simon and my daed."

All of her muscles tensed. She couldn't cry. Wouldn't let him see how much he affected her. But the back of her throat burned.

Why did God have to take Daniel? Why did He have to make Joseph so sick? And why had He brought Elam back?

"Fine, I'll think about it."

Chapter Four

Naomi lifted her face to the sun and breathed in the scent of warming earth. Mamm, about to make an oatmeal pie, had found herself out of brown sugar. With Joseph down for a nap and the weather this warm and beautiful, Naomi offered to walk to the bulk food store. What she didn't tell Mamm was how perfect the timing was. She and Elam had a meeting with Sylvia to pick up the information Simon had put together for the auction.

She hadn't found the courage yet to tell her parents she was working with Elam. Forcing the words through her lips shouldn't be this hard. But she held back. They would not approve of her spending time with him, though they had no basis for worry. She would never let him worm his way into her life again. Once this auction was over, she would steer clear of him for the rest of her life. She would have to tell them sooner or later. Nothing stayed secret for very long here. But she would hold off as long as she could.

A slight breeze tugged at her dress. She shouldn't enjoy this taste of freedom as much as she did, but every now and again, it was nice to not be Naomi the widow, Naomi the mother of a child with special needs, Naomi the bakery employee, but just Naomi. As a small blue car whizzed by, she jumped to the side of the road.

In a few days, the early daffodils would be in full bloom. Tulips' leaves peeked above the ground. The buds lining the tree's twigs were about to burst open. Spring.

Amid the back-and-forth calls of the cardinals in the trees came the clip-clop of a horse's hooves. Which of her neighbors was out and about? She turned and groaned. *Nein.* Not him.

Elam held the horse's reins in one hand and waved at her, a smile deepening the creases around his mouth. "*Gut morgan*, Naomi. I'm glad I found you." He slowed Prancer, his shiny black buggy horse, to keep pace with her. "I stopped at your house to pick you up, and your mamm told me you had left already.

She said you were on your way to the store, but she didn't know about the meeting."

Naomi sucked in her breath. "You told Mamm about it? You had no right to do that."

He pushed back his straw hat. "How was I supposed to know you didn't tell her?"

"Well, I mean, you should have, it's just that…" She sighed. Elam was right. She shouldn't have kept that information from her parents. But when she got home, she would have to see the double disappointment on their faces. "Fine. You weren't at fault. But I didn't ask for a ride."

"I know you didn't, but I thought it might be nice."

She kept walking.

"Naomi."

The clicking of the horse's hooves behind her halted. Elam's footsteps approached. "Come on. You can't stop talking to me forever."

"*Ja*, I can."

"See, you already spoke three words."

Despite herself, the corners of her mouth turned up. He always did have this way of making her smile, of keeping her from being too serious. That's one of the things she loved about him. *Had loved.* Didn't love anymore. But he did have a point. She stopped. "Fine.

You win this time. It would be silly of me to walk when you're going that way."

Once they were both settled in the closed buggy, Elam clicked to the horse, and they trotted off. Several times, she caught him glancing at her from the corner of his eyes. Finally, she had to say something. "What do you keep looking at?"

"Can we agree to be civil to each other? At least while we work on the auction."

"I'm always polite."

"Glad to hear that." His words were clipped and short. Had she offended him? How, by being cordial?

She didn't have time to mull over the thought as they arrived at the bakery. They slipped around to the back, went up the stairs and knocked on the door. Sylvia answered, a few salt-and-pepper hairs escaping from under her *kapp*. "*Ach*, how *gut* to see both of you. I was just dozing off, so forgive how I look. Let me put the kettle on for some tea."

Even though Elam entered, Naomi stood firm in the doorway. "We're sorry to disturb you. Please, go back to your nap. You must be exhausted."

Sylvia waved her in. "Nonsense. The place is too quiet without Simon. I just sat down with my sewing to give my old bones a rest, and I can't keep my eyes open."

"How is he doing?" Naomi brushed shoulders with Elam as she entered, a shiver racing through her. Once inside, she stood a few feet away from him.

"Grumbling that the hospital meals aren't as good as mine and that the nurses don't let him sleep. In other words, he's much like his old self." A twinkle sparkled in Sylvia's blue eyes. "Another few days there, and then he'll be my problem. Now, Simon had something he wanted me to give the two of you. Sit at the table, and I'll be right back."

She hustled out of the room as Elam and Naomi took their seats, Sylvia's basket of needles and thread on the table, small scissors and a pair of pants beside it. Naomi shifted her feet. "We shouldn't be bothering her."

"She told us to come. We won't stay long, just enough to get Simon's notes. I do have another surprise for you, though." He winked, and her cheeks burned. Why did her insides flutter when he played so coy with her? Daniel had been gone only a little over a year.

Naomi rose, drew an old, stained mug from the cabinet and set about making tea. Even if they wouldn't stay to enjoy it, Sylvia would benefit from a cup.

Before the kettle whistled, Sylvia lumbered in, a large cardboard box in her hands. "Oh dear, I didn't realize how heavy this was." She plunked it on the table, worn from many family and community meals.

Elam stood and peered inside. "What is all this?"

"Everything Simon says you'll need to finish the preparations for the auction. You'll find his contacts for the auction house, the list of donated items and whatever else you might have to have. I don't know exactly the full contents. He always handled every little detail, so you might have quite a job on your hands figuring out what is what and what you need to do."

Naomi brought over the steaming cup of tea. The sweet fragrance of chamomile was homey. Her muscles, tense since Elam had driven up behind her, relaxed. She set the mug in front of Sylvia. "Elam will get it straight. Don't you or Simon worry about a thing. Enjoy your tea, and we'll leave you in peace."

"You've only just come."

"And now we must go. We have Aaron's old wheelchair, the one he used before he got the motorized version, so if your husband needs it, let us know."

"*Denki.* You really are too good to an old woman like me. And you, too, Elam, for doing this."

"I'm grateful to Simon for giving me a chance to get back into the district's good graces."

They said their goodbyes, Elam carried the box out and Naomi started down the driveway so she could get to the grocery store.

"Hey, where are you going?" Elam made his way around the Englisch in their usual long line for baked goods.

"I told you. Mamm needs brown sugar."

"But I'm going to take you to see a surprise. Have you already forgotten?"

In the same way the women ogled the new baby in church, the Englisch watched Elam and Naomi. She squirmed under the intense scrutiny. This is why she didn't really want to speak with the papers. She didn't want to be any more of a spectacle to the Englisch.

With no other choice, she marched to where Elam waited with his buggy. When she got close enough, she hissed at him. "In the future, please refrain from shouting at me in public. Or anytime at all. I have to be on my way. Joseph will wake from his nap and be ready to eat."

"I won't keep you long, I promise. When

we're finished, I'll run you to the store and then home. You'll be back sooner than you would have been had you walked everywhere."

Maybe if she gave him what he wanted, she could be rid of him faster.

Probably not.

With a sigh, she climbed into the buggy.

After a short ride from the bakery, Elam reined Prancer to a halt near a tree on the far side of the parking lot in front of the large, rectangular red-and-silver metal pole barn used for auctions. Most of the time, the Englisch used it to sell their produce.

Naomi hadn't cracked a smile since they left the Herschbergers'. And she pulled her frown down farther as they sat in the buggy and stared at the building. What could he do to get her to grin? "What do you think of my surprise?"

"I'm supposed to be surprised?"

"You didn't think I'd bring you here, did you?"

"As far as surprises go, it's about as good as an unplanned root canal."

A hearty chuckle burst from Elam, and even Naomi gave a soft laugh. *Ach*, so much more like it. "Point taken. Next time I surprise you with something, it will be better. I promise."

"Why are we here?"

"Because my mind has been whirring since Simon asked us to finish the plans for the auction. I have so many ideas, but I need your help." He jumped from the buggy.

Naomi climbed down before he could assist her. "There's not much to do. We set up the bakery items over there, the plants and such here, the tools there and everything else inside. Like it's always been done."

"That's fine, as far as it goes, but we have to think bigger and grander if we want to raise more money. Like maybe having one of those shaved ice trucks I've seen at the county fairs. If it's a hot, sunny day, that should bring in an extra boost of cash."

"I'm not sure. Shouldn't we limit our offerings to Amish-produced items? Isn't that why the Englisch come? They can get shaved ice everywhere."

"But it would be a big seller. We have to continue to add new offerings and change things around, or we won't get repeat customers from year to year."

She shook her head and pulled her eyebrows into a deep V. "While it's fine to search for ways to improve the auction and increase proceeds, those who come are looking for a uniquely Amish experience. They wouldn't appreciate seeing a vendor they could find at any county fair. We've always done things the same way, and it's always worked. Have you changed so much you don't remember?"

He huffed. Naomi was the most stubborn woman he'd ever met. Time hadn't changed that. "Can't you see how *gut* this will be for the auction?"

"And slowly, you'll take away everything Amish about it until it's like any other craft fair. I think including a silent auction for those who don't like to bid with others watching is a much better idea."

"And I think I'm going to find out how we go about getting a shaved ice truck."

"Whatever you want to do is fine with me." She waved as if dismissing him. "You have my blessing. Can we go now?"

He deflated a little. "I thought you'd be more excited."

"This is your project, not mine."

"Why won't you help me?"

She faced him, red blooming on her cheeks. "Why not? You're kidding me. You really don't know the answer to that question? Let me tick off the reasons for you. My brother and his permanent disability. Your leaving me. My humiliation in the district when you took off. Isn't that enough?"

He stepped back. "It was an accident, Naomi, nothing more than that. I never set out to harm your brother. Or you." Maybe putting this together with her wasn't the best idea in the world. But like it or not, they were stuck on the project. "I was young and foolish. And scared. And you turned your back to me, refused to even listen to me. But as we work together, you'll see I've grown up. Give me the chance to show you that I'm not the same man who left three years ago." His heart banged in his chest.

She paced in small circles, her focus on the gravel at her feet. "I'm sorry to have gotten so angry with you." She kicked at a stone with her bare feet.

"Can we put aside our differences long enough to make this work? Neither of us wants to go to Sylvia or Simon and tell them we can't do it."

"You're right."

"Does that mean you'll partner with me?"

"Partner, no. Give you a helping hand from time to time, fine. I give up, because you'll pester me until I agree."

The way she said it was almost like he was a bully. "I don't want to pressure you."

"I said fine. I'll make sure the quilts come in and get organized, along with the donated items. And arrange the bakery sales. What else?"

He sighed. One major obstacle overcame. They spent the next few minutes reviewing a list of items that needed to be taken care of, one he'd written up last night while the gas lamp hissed overhead. With the box from Simon, the list was sure to grow.

"Is that enough for now? I don't want to overwhelm you since you have Joseph to look after and your job."

"That will be *gut*. I'll let you know when I have this finished."

"One more thing. The papers. You never answered me if you would go to the press and share Joseph's story with them. It's sure to bring in many more tourists. The story is moving and should compel the Englisch to come and buy our products. Raise more money."

Naomi rubbed her prayer *kapp* string between her fingers. "There are so many needs in the district right now. Like Simon. He'll need help, too. And your daed."

"All the more reason to sell as much as we can. What harm will it do? We'll tell them no pictures. No Englischer will even know it's you."

"They won't?"

"If the paper wants the story, they'll have to publish it anonymously."

"They'd do that?"

"I believe they would."

She scrunched up her forehead. "Can I give you my answer in a few days? I have to think."

"Sure. But don't wait too long. We'll need time for the interviews and for people to make their plans." A streak of lightning and a quick crack of thunder brought Elam's attention to the sky. When had the thick, black clouds rolled in? A gust of wind pulled his straw hat from his head and sent it skittering across the parking lot. He gave chase to it, several more bolts of lightning brightening the now-dusky afternoon.

He and Naomi raced for the buggy. She fell behind.

"Ah." Her cry cut through the rolling thunder. "Elam."

He turned. She'd fallen, her bare shin scratched and bloodied. The first fat drops of water fell to the gravel. He hurried and helped her up. While they ran, he kept a hold of her, the rain pelting them. They finally reached the buggy, the fierce wind buffeting it, and it swayed side to side. Now soaked to the skin, they climbed aboard.

Naomi shivered, and he pulled her to himself. They used to be close like this.

A streak of light. A deafening crack. The ground shook.

Kaboom.

Naomi shrieked.

The tree they were next to split in half and crashed to the earth, missing the buggy to each side.

She trembled in his arms.

He held her close and whispered against her cheek. "Hush now. We're safe."

But would his heart ever be?

Chapter Five

Only the clinking of silverware on the dinner plates broke the silence around the Yoders' large farmhouse table. Mamm loaded Daed's plate with another heap of creamed corn. He grasped his fork with his left hand, his right one paralyzed by the stroke, and tried to shovel the vegetable into his mouth.

Much of it ended up back on the plate or in his lap. He grunted, the right of his mouth downturned. "Can't even eat properly." He thunked his fork onto his dish, pushed away from the table and reached for his walker.

Elam jumped to his feet and grasped his daed by the elbow to help him to stand.

Daed shook him off. "I don't need your help. I'm capable of getting out of a chair."

"I just thought it would be easier..."

"Easier. That's what you always want, isn't it?"

Elam scrunched his eyebrows as he stared at his daed. When had the lines formed around his eyes? When had he become an old man? "I don't understand what you mean."

"You run away when times get hard. Now you're back, but for how long? A week? A month? A year?"

"You know I'm back to stay. I came to give you a hand until Isaac returns, but I'm not leaving the district again."

"I don't need your help. We could manage just fine."

Mamm shook her head as she carried the dishes to the sink. "*Nein*, we weren't managing at all until Elam came home. How would the crops get planted if not for him? Don't be a foolish old man. We need his help." She turned and smiled over her shoulder. "He came on his own, volunteered to do this. Let's not turn him away."

Elam sucked in a breath. Is that what Daed wanted to do? Open the door and give him a shove outside?

"Nobody said anything about that." The muscles on the good side of Daed's face strained as he pulled himself to a standing position. "Just didn't ask for his help." He shuffled out of the kitchen, the back door slamming behind him.

Mamm returned to the table with a dishrag in one hand. She patted Elam's cheek. "Don't be so glum. I hate to see you sad like this." Many laugh lines crinkled around her eyes and mouth. Over the years, she had plenty to be happy about. And plenty of heartaches to cry over.

"He barely tolerates my being here. Even across the table from me at dinner, he glances my way only when necessary. When Isaac returns, he'll be happier."

"That's not true. He loves you."

"You can't convince me."

"He's afraid he's going to lose you again. He couldn't stand that, you know."

"Why does no one believe that I'm staying put?"

"Give them time to see you're sincere. When troubles come and you face them head-on, then they'll trust you."

"And can they forgive me? Forget the past?"

Her face softened, and she stared at a spot behind him. "That I cannot answer for anyone else."

When she set to washing the dishes, he wandered outside, the early spring evening cool. Daed wasn't on the porch. Where could he have gone? In the short time Elam had been home, he'd built a ramp so Daed didn't have to negotiate the stairs. Mamm had thanked him. Daed had not.

A light shone from one of the barn's windows, the one that held Daed's office. Elam walked down the porch steps, across the dusty yard and into the barn, the odors of hay and cows as familiar to him as the smells of Mamm's apple pie. The animals munched their dinner, lowing songs to each other. On a bale in the far corner, the new litter of kittens mewed.

He entered the office through the open door, Daed at the desk, scratching in the account books with a pencil, his lips drawn tight as he struggled to use his left hand.

"Do you have a few minutes?"

Daed grunted, not even glancing at Elam. "What is it you want?" Even with therapy, his speech remained slurred.

"I'll do those figures for you later."

"I'm capable. There may be much I can't do anymore, but writing is one thing I can. And figuring numbers."

"I just thought…" This was getting off to a terrible beginning. Best to start over. "What do you have against me?"

"Nothing. You're my son. But sometimes, I

wonder. You always were…" Daed squeezed his eyes shut and furrowed his brow. Sometimes he couldn't recall the word he needed.

"Independent."

"*Ja*, and stubborn and strong-willed. What are you doing here? Why did you truly come back?"

Elam's windpipe tightened. "I missed this place and the people. And it was time to stop running, to face up to what I did. I didn't realize that making amends would be so hard."

"You can't walk back into people's lives and expect them to let go of what happened like that. You—" Daed pointed straight at Elam's heart "—have to prove yourself."

Isn't that what he'd been doing? How long was it going to take? So far, he hadn't made headway with anyone. Including Naomi.

"Time and hard work. That's what you need."

Had Daed heard his thoughts? Elam puffed out a breath, then spun on his heel and left the office and the barn. He stood in the farmyard and stared at the multitude of stars in the sky. In the city lights of Madison, they got lost. Here, they were almost close enough to touch.

In order to show the people of the district he wasn't the man who left, he would have to start with Aaron's family. Already, he had upset Naomi. He shouldn't have dismissed her objections to the shaved ice the way he had. If he admitted so to her, perhaps they could work together better.

Aaron sat in a wheelchair for the rest of his life. If that's the amount of time it took for Elam to make amends for the accident, then that's how long he would work for it.

Naomi pressed her nose against the window of Frank's van. Joseph was peacefully sleeping in the car seat beside her. In her hand, she held the information for his surgery. The one he needed sooner rather than later, according to the information the doctor had just shared. Naomi leaned over her son and whispered. "Dear God, protect my baby. Make him strong. Make me strong. Help us get through this."

Elam was correct. This year, there were many medical needs in the district. Much as she hated to admit it, she had to work with him on the auction. He was going to bring Simon's box and meet her at her home to go through it. She would have to be as nice to him as possible. They would get nothing done if they argued.

She rubbed her upper arms. The way Elam held her during the storm warmed her through and through. For a brief glimmer of time, she was safe. Cared for. He watched out for her.

But Aaron would always be a reminder of what happened that night Elam betrayed her trust. He'd broken her brother's body and her heart. She wouldn't let Elam back into her life. No matter that Simon threw them together to organize the auction.

Maybe Elam did have a point about the papers, though. Perhaps if she gave them an interview, people would be interested and would come from all over the state to the auction.

Her palms dampened at the thought of having to talk to the reporters. What would they ask her? What would she say?

Just as Frank turned into the driveway, Elam pulled his buggy in behind them. She unbuckled Joseph's car seat and stepped out with a wave to Frank.

Elam came toward them and tickled Joseph's tummy, and the now-awake *bobbeli* squealed. "I hope the doctor had nothing but good things to say."

"She said it was time to schedule the surgery. He's going to have it in July."

"That's *gut*, isn't it?" He grasped one of his black suspenders.

"*Ja*, I suppose." So why did her head ache?

He touched her arm. She stepped away. "Please, don't."

Nein, she couldn't rely on him for help and comfort. But her chest ached. Some nights, alone in her room, she cried herself to sleep. How much lonelier it would be when she moved to the *dawdi haus*. "Come in. We can start sorting through the papers."

He grabbed the box from his buggy and followed her into the house. Mamm took Joseph and Naomi and Elam settled at the table, the large box between them.

He cleared his throat, and she gazed at him. An uneven red flush mottled his neck. "First of all, I want to apologize for the other day."

"You...you do?" Why did her stomach dip the way it did?

"*Ja*. I shouldn't have dismissed your ideas the way I did. That was inconsiderate of me. You make a *gut* point. This is an Amish auction, not an Englisch one. All the other items we offer come from our communities. We should forget the shaved ice truck."

"Having a hard time finding a vendor?" She flashed him a playful grin.

The red creeped into his cheeks. "Well, now that you mention it." He chuckled, his coloring returning to normal. "I'm not incapable of seeing reason. You were right. I was wrong."

Warmth seeped into her chest. The old Elam rarely admitted his mistakes. "*Denki* for your apology. Offering a cold treat on a warm day was a nice thought. Is there an alternative to the shaved ice?"

Elam stroked his clean-shaven cheek. "Your family makes the best ice cream I've ever had. Just vanilla, but there is a secret ingredient in there, say not?"

"There is, but you want to make ice cream? How are we going have enough for all those people?"

"That's a good question."

"Multiple machines hooked up to generators?"

He grinned, and her arms broke out in gooseflesh. She focused on the pencil in her hand.

"That's a great idea. Maybe someone in the district has a large-capacity churn."

"I'll ask around at the church service next week."

For a long while, they sorted through the papers, Naomi jotting notes on a yellow legal pad, filling several pages with people they needed to contact, payments that had to be made and ideas they had.

She could almost close her eyes and imagine that the past three years hadn't happened. Almost. His deep voice washed over her and lulled her.

Elam's words broke into her into thoughts. "I'd like to make some furniture pieces for the auction. I was hoping your daed would let me use his equipment. I have an Englisch friend who has a workshop in his garage, but I want to construct them the true Amish way."

If Daed allowed Elam to work here, she would run into him every day, just as she had when he was Daed's employee. Did her hands tremble because of dread or excitement? She had to say something to him, but what? Surely not that she was happy he'd be so close. "Well, I hope the meeting with him goes well. I think we've reached the end of the stuff in the box. I should feed Joseph before he fusses."

Elam rose and filed the papers away. "And what about the newspapers?"

She locked her knees to keep them from knocking together. "Go ahead and contact the reporters. I'll speak to them."

"I have the letters ready to put in the mail. Would you like to read them first?"

"*Nein*. Just send them." Before she changed her mind.

Chapter Six

The tang of pine and the sweetness of maple permeated the shed where Leroy Bontrager ran his woodworking shop. As Elam made his way through the building, he glided his hand down a length of quarter-sawn oak that had been sanded to a mirror-like smoothness. The whir of the gas-powered table saw welcomed him home. *Ja*, this is where he belonged. Construction, as he'd done while away, was building. Woodworking was creating.

"Hello, Leroy, are you here?"

Naomi's father entered the main room from the back. He wiped dark stain from his fingers onto what must have been an old shirt. The heady odor of varnish hung about him. "Elam. Why are you here?"

Not the start he'd been hoping for given that first meeting between them. Maybe this wasn't the best idea. "You're hard at work, as always." Several kitchen chairs sat in a row along one wall, as did a couple of book-shelves and a large dining room table with well-turned legs.

"Of course."

"Daed told me you hired Solomon Mast to help after I left."

"Aaron gives me a hand as much as he can, doing a few things from his chair. But I can't run this place with the two of us. Solomon is a *gut* man, but still learning. He puts in a hard day's work, and I appreciate that. But he doesn't have the eye, the insight that you..."

Had Leroy been about to compliment him? "Naomi and I have been working on the auction. She said they've set the date for Joseph's surgery."

"That's *gut.*" Leroy dug in his pants pocket, but didn't produce anything. "Then the boy can grow strong. I can teach him to sweep the floors and get me my tools. Maybe to do a little staining."

"That was always my least favorite part of the job." Elam chuckled.

Leroy didn't. "I have an order due tomorrow that I have to finish. What can I help you with? You didn't come here to make idle chatter."

Elam swallowed hard. "You're right. I don't

want to take up your valuable time. I'd like to build some things for the auction for Joseph's—" Elam drew in a deep breath "—and Aaron's medical expenses. Could I use your equipment? Your saw and sander and things like that. In off-hours, of course."

Leroy stroked his graying beard, his eyes narrow.

"When I ran away, I left you in the lurch, down an employee. And I caused your family a great deal of suffering and pain. What I did was foolish. Stupid. I can't go back and undo my mistakes, but I would like to move forward. To somehow make up for the accident. And for breaking Naomi's heart."

Leroy took a seat in a rocking chair, one with simple rungs along the back. As he examined Elam, he rocked.

Elam's throat closed so he had a difficult time drawing a breath. "Please, I'm asking for your forgiveness."

Leroy shot to his feet, the chair still moving behind him. "Forgiveness? That's what you want? The Amish way is to forgive, and so I have. *Ja*, right away, in my heart, I forgave you. But forgetting. That is another matter. Every time I help my son in and out of his chair, I remember. Every time his mother massages his useless legs, we remember.

Every time I see the sadness in my daughter's eyes, I remember."

Elam hunched his shoulders and rubbed his temples. "For a long time, I avoided my problems, thought they would disappear if I wasn't around to see what I had done. Life doesn't work that way, though. The accident, Aaron's condition, my promise to Naomi, all those weighed on my mind every day. I'm glad you forgave me. And I understand that you can't forget. But if we could only move forward. Repair the damage between us."

Leroy fisted his right hand and pounded on the table. "Repair the damage? Can you fix my son's broken back so he can walk again? Not even the Englisch doctors with all their fancy medicines and expensive therapy can do that. He will never take another step again. Never. And what about his chances of marrying and having a family? Do you realize you've robbed him of that, too?"

Elam staggered back three steps. His chest burned. "What can I do to make it up to you?" The whispered question reverberated in the room.

"There is nothing."

"Daed, I need to flip that end table so I can finish staining it." Aaron rolled in from the back room.

Leroy narrowed his eyes, his jaw tight. "And he can't do it because of you."

A weight crushed Elam's chest. "I know." He turned to Aaron and strode toward the back. "Let me help you."

The heaviness of Leroy's stare pressed on Elam's shoulders, but he didn't flinch. Instead, he followed Aaron to the staining room. "Can I ever make it up to you?"

Aaron pointed to the half-stained table. "I don't hate you."

"Glad to hear that." Still, the young man didn't even glance in Elam's direction. "I shouldn't have done what I did. It's my carelessness that put you here. That stole your life from you." He struggled to draw a breath.

"This is my life now. I have to accept it. Nothing will change it."

In other words, nothing Elam could ever do would be enough. He stared at Aaron's atrophied legs. His stomach clenched. He moved the table.

"You're a talented young man. I've seen your work. Your injuries shouldn't prevent you from doing what you love." He shifted his weight from one foot to the other. "I'll be going. See you later."

When he reached the doorway, he turned. Aaron reached for a can of varnish on a shelf just out of his grasp. He pushed himself up, but it wasn't quite enough.

He couldn't manage a simple task like taking something from a shelf. Elam returned to Aaron and handed him the can.

"Denki."

"Anytime. And I mean that. If there is ever anything I can do..." But what would there be? He left the shop and made his way back to the buggy.

The home's screen door slammed, and Naomi descended the porch steps toward him. "How did it go? Is Daed going to let you use the equipment?"

Elam shrugged. "I didn't stick around long enough for him to answer. He says he's forgiven me but can't forget."

"Forgetting is impossible."

Could he ever change their minds?

The next afternoon, Naomi tiptoed down the stairs, then held her breath as one she stepped on creaked. After twenty minutes of rocking, her very tired *bobbeli* had finally given up the fight and drifted to sleep. A few seconds passed. No sound from the bedroom she shared with her son. *Gut*, she hadn't wakened him.

The kitchen sat quiet. Mamm had mentioned working in the garden this morning. From the counter, Naomi drew the wooden box that held all of Mamm's recipes printed on three-by-five cards in her own neat script. Many bore stains from the ingredients used in them. With twenty-five years of cooking and baking to her credit, Mamm didn't often use the recipes anymore.

Where was that one for ice cream? Naomi should have memorized it herself, but couldn't remember how much of the special vanilla it called for, the secret ingredient Elam mentioned when they decided to make this instead of the shaved ice.

The back door clicked open and shut, and Naomi peered up as Mamm entered the kitchen, wiping her dirty hands on her apron. "What do you need from there?"

"The recipe for ice cream. I can't find it in my own box, and I'm not seeing it in yours."

"It should be in there."

Naomi rifled through the cards but still couldn't locate it. "How much vanilla?"

"Two tablespoons, one of each flavor."

"*Denki.* Now I have to multiply that by how many ever batches we're going to make for the auction before I run to the store to make sure Marlin can order it and get it here in time. And everything else we need."

Mamm pumped water at the sink and scrubbed her hands. "Daed and I have been talking about this auction and your working with Elam. We don't like it. Remember how you felt when he walked away? He hurt your brother and broke your heart. It's not *gut* for you to spend so much time with him."

A lifetime had passed since she had harbored any feelings for Elam. *Ja*, she had been devastated when he'd left, not willing to stay and face what he'd done, not willing to fight for a future with her. But now she was older and wiser. This time, she would guard her heart better and wouldn't lose herself to his charm.

"Naomi, have you heard anything I've said?"

Mamm's question snapped Naomi to the present. "Don't worry. I'm not the same naive seventeen-year-old I was when I fell in love with him. Joseph is my main priority. And the only reason I'm working on this auction. Simon volunteered us without asking, and I couldn't turn him down."

"Daed doesn't want to forbid you." Mamm futzed with untying her apron, her back to Naomi.

She couldn't have heard right. "Forbid me? From what?"

"Seeing that boy."

"He's hardly a child. Nor am I."

"Just because you're an adult doesn't mean you can sass your mamm. You're under your daed's protection once more. Elam's actions tore him apart. He loves you so much and doesn't want to see that kind of pain in your eyes again."

"They're making progress on the *dawdi haus*. Soon, I'll be back on my own." Maybe having her freedom again wouldn't be such a bad thing.

"But you still need someone to watch out for you." Mamm turned to face her, faint lines fanning from the corners of her eyes. The cares of the world etched those wrinkles.

Naomi scraped the chair back and stood, her chest and cheeks warm. She bit back words stronger than her earlier ones. Working hard to keep from stomping across the kitchen, she marched outside. The screen door banged behind her, maybe a little too hard.

Life wasn't fair. It wasn't fair that Elam left her. That Daniel died. That her parents treated her like she was still a child.

Out in the farmyard, she kicked at a stone on the gravel driveway. Her breath came in small gasps. Sure, working with Elam on the auction hadn't been her idea, but she had made a commitment. And despite her parents trying to tell her what to do, she had to see this through.

Chapter Seven

Naomi pushed Daed's favorite brown chair into the first-floor bedroom and then shoved the couch along the living room wall, as out of the way as possible. She had fed Joseph, but he hadn't nursed long before he fell asleep. And he had struggled to get the milk into his tummy, breathing hard, sweating.

If only the surgery day would hurry and get here. But then again, if it would just take its time in coming. She could lose her son.

She shook the thoughts away. The women would be here in a few minutes to finish this quilt for the auction. Every spare second she had between the bakery and Joseph, Naomi worked on the list of items that needed to be done. She had sketched out where everything would take place and was compiling the list of donations. Many nights during the past week, she had worked until Daed turned out the lamp over the table.

The roasted scent of coffee filled the kitchen as she entered. Mamm drizzled a glaze on the coffee cake while Laura pulled a batch of oatmeal cookies from the oven. Naomi swiped one and popped it in her mouth. "I'll get Sam to help me set up the form, but is there anything else you need?"

Mamm motioned to the cabinet next to the sink. "You could set out the plates and silverware. Laura, when you finish there, go find your brother. I saw him heading to the barn not too long ago, probably to pester those poor cats."

Naomi got busy with the chore Mamm gave her. "I'm sorry about storming out the other day."

"I'm sorry about what I said. Sometimes it's easy for me to forget you're a grown woman." Mamm hugged her. "I know none of this has been easy, especially with Elam back. We have to trust that you know what you're doing. Your daed and I can't forbid you from doing what you feel is right."

"*Denki*, Mamm. You do have so much wisdom to impart, and I need to keep that in mind."

Mamm drew away and untied her apron. "Well, now, we'd best finish getting ready."

Before long, feminine voices and laughter floated from outside as the quilting party arrived in several buggy loads. Sam came in among them and set up the frame while the girls and ladies enjoyed a cup of coffee. Before they even sat to work, Joseph cried.

Naomi hurried to his room. She picked him up, his few curls damp with sweat. "Oh, my *bobbeli*, don't tell me you're getting another fever." He nestled against her neck and cried all the harder.

His cheek was cool against her skin. "What is it, little one? So unhappy you are." She walked the small room with him, but it took a good five minutes to quiet him. "And now you're awake, so I don't know how much quilting I'll get done."

She brought him from the bedroom, patting his back to stop his wailing. "Look who wanted to join the party."

The women rushed to him, fawning over her *bobbeli*, who gave a contented yawn. Were his lips bluer than usual? Was his heart condition getting worse? *Nein*, it must just be the blue from her dress. Sylvia took him from her arms and cooed over him.

Talk swirled around Naomi. "Have you heard how Leah Byler is getting along with her twins? *Ach*, I can't imagine having two toddlers and two infants at the same time."

"What are you planning for your garden this year?"

"Simon came home from the rehab center yesterday, say not? Must be good to have him home."

"I've heard tell that you and Elam were seen riding in a buggy together the other day."

At that statement Naomi stood up straight. "He took me to the store so we could order what we needed for the ice cream."

"So it's true, that the two of you are working together." Bethel Byler shook her head as her bony fingers pulled her needle through the fabric.

Naomi gulped as each of the fifteen ladies stared at her. "Simon Herschberger asked us to help. I couldn't turn him down."

Fourteen pairs of lips tightened. All but Sylvia's. "Naomi has been so sweet to our family since Simon's accident. She checks in every time she works at the bakery and swept my floor the other day when my back was giving me trouble. In all my life, I've never run into such a helpful young woman."

Maybe a hole would open in the wood floor and Naomi could fall through to the cold, spider-filled basement. Anything would be preferable to this. "Really, it's nothing. I'm glad I can do it."

"I, for one, don't know how you can stand to be around Elam so much," Eva Miller said as she bent over her work, the set of her jaw firm.

"It's not like I volunteered or—"

Joseph's wails saved her from having to defend herself. She grabbed her *bobbeli* from Sylvia and swung around to hide in the kitchen.

Too bad Elam stood in the doorway, blocking her path.

Fourteen gasps sounded behind her. And her traitorous heart missed a beat.

"Hello, Naomi." Elam's voice was low and tight.

She needed that hole in the floor more than ever. Surely he had heard some of what the women had said.

"Hello there, young man." Elam rubbed the top of Joseph's head, and the child calmed.

She backed up a few steps to put some distance between them. "Joseph's fussy, and I have to—"

"He doesn't look the least bit upset to me." Elam waved a piece of paper in front of Naomi. "I came to bring you some news."

Joseph had to pick that moment to gaze at

Elam and break into a toothless grin. Naomi sighed. Just when this day couldn't get any worse. "What is it?"

"The Eau Claire and Madison papers wrote back to us. They both want to interview you. And the best of all? The Milwaukee paper wants to do a feature. A big spread in their Sunday edition."

The women behind Naomi murmured. "What is he talking about? Newspapers? Big-city Englisch ones?"

Naomi's mouth went dry. How could he have blurted out the news in front of everyone? "I… You shouldn't… I mean…"

She clung to her child and fled up the stairs.

Elam stood in the living room's doorway, gazing at the staircase where Naomi disappeared. Why had she run away? Why wasn't she willing to listen?

A gaggle of women, all seated around a quilting frame, stared at him as if he'd grown a mane and a tail. "I… I…" Speechless wasn't his usual condition.

One of the older women, Ruth Zook, the bishop's nosy spinster sister, scraped her chair back and marched to stand in front of him. She wagged her arthritic finger. "Just who do you think you are, barging in here, upsetting that poor, sweet girl? Hasn't she been through enough? And what is this about newspaper interviews?" She shook her head. "Being away hasn't taught you anything. You always were one to charge ahead and do whatever you wanted without thinking about it."

He wiped his damp hands on his broadcloth pants. "She agreed to speak to the reporters to bring more buyers to the auction—the one that's raising money for her son's surgery. And we plan to do it anonymously. No one will know who she is, just what the funds that the auction generates is used for."

Naomi's mamm shook her head. "I don't want to see my daughter hurt more than she already is. Isn't it enough that she's working long hours to help you?"

Sylvia stood and sidled next to Ruth. "Simon asked Elam and Naomi to finish organizing the auction for him. He trusted Elam with this job, so let him do what Simon has asked, whatever he feels is best."

Ruth puffed out her cheeks, expelled the air and whirled to take her seat.

"*Denki*, Sylvia." Without her and Simon, he wouldn't have anyone in the district on his side. He owed them a great debt. Elam lowered his voice. "I don't know what I did to send Naomi running like that." He rubbed the ache in his chest.

"She is a young mother with a very sick *bobbeli*. That's emotional. Be kind and supportive. She needs you more than she realizes she does." Sylvia patted his upper arm before returning to the rest of the women.

Elam's head swam as he left the house. Naomi should have been happy about the newspaper interviews. They had talked about it. She'd agreed to speak to the reporters. Had she changed her mind?

He kicked at a larger stone in the gravel driveway on the way to his buggy. He'd have to talk to her later, when the rest of the women had gone home.

Elam hitched Prancer and gave a half-hearted cluck to the horse, who then plodded down the street. He didn't go directly home, but meandered the quiet country roads. Gray clouds hung low in the sky, and a chilly wind buffeted the bravest of the daffodils.

When he paid attention to where he was, he found himself down a dirt road and at Miller's pond. He'd come here every chance he'd gotten as a boy, a fishing pole in one hand and a Styrofoam container of worms in the other. Large trees surrounded the small lake, a few weeping willows dipping their branches into the pond. A foggy mist rose from the water's surface. A large, smooth rock sat at the pond's shore. The kissing rock, most people called it. Many young Amish had their first kisses here, stolen pecks on the cheek as early teens.

He had been among them. Naomi had been the one and only girl he'd ever loved. He doubled over and rubbed his head under his hat. Young, cocky, a braggart, he thought nothing bad would ever touch him. Though he dabbled in the Englisch world by buying a truck and a cell phone, he intended to join the church, marry Naomi and settle into the way of life his ancestors had lived for hundreds of years.

And then that one night happened.

Nothing would ever be the same. Had he been a fool to come home? A fool to believe the district would welcome him with open arms? *Ja*, probably. What was he doing here other than torturing himself and everyone around him?

No doubt, many in the district believed it would be better if he left, if he went his own way. Isaac would be home soon.

The auction. He had promised Simon he would organize it. And so he would.

But after that…

The temptation to run pulled at him. But if

he left, he would never have the chance to re-deem himself. Or to gain Naomi's forgiveness. What was the right thing to do?

Chapter Eight

As Naomi stood at the kitchen window washing the lunch dishes, Mamm wrapped her in an embrace. She sank into Mamm's arms.

"You're exhausted. I heard Joseph crying several times last night."

Naomi sighed. "He's hungry, but he isn't feeding well. He struggles so for breath." Her voice caught. "He needs that surgery. Soon."

"Stay home from the bakery tomorrow and rest. You don't need to be on your feet for so long after walking the floor all night with a sick child. Sylvia will understand."

"Sylvia has her hands full with Simon home. And now that the weather is nice, the busy season is starting. She can't spare me."

"And here comes another one of your obligations. After what happened the other day, you'd think he'd be too ashamed of himself to show up here."

Naomi peered out the window. Elam un-hitched Prancer, led him to graze in the field and made his way to the house. That's right, they had to sign the contracts with the auction house and order the tents they would need. But after the reaction of the women to her going to the papers, her midsection clenched. She smoothed down her apron and cringed at the streaks of raspberry jam down the front of it from the sandwiches she had made. Well, she didn't have time to change, so it would have to do. She hustled to the door and let in Elam.

He lugged a large box and plunked it on the kitchen table. When she crossed her arms in front of her, he sobered. "First things first. I want to apologize for the other day, when I blurted our news in front of the other women. I know what a private person you are, and I shouldn't have done that. The letter from the Milwaukee paper had me excited, and I didn't contain it well. Can you forgive me?"

"You're always asking for forgiveness."

"Will you give it?"

"It doesn't matter. I'm not going to speak to them."

He creased his forehead. "But we talked

about this. For your son, Naomi, and your brother, and all the others, you have to tell your story. I promise to be with you every step of the way. They won't use your name or anything. No one will know it's you. One article in each newspaper, and it will be over. Think about your family."

"That's all I think about. My son is very, very sick. He's not sleeping well. He needs that surgery." She clenched her jaw.

"Even more reason to go through with the interviews. I have the meetings set up. To make it easy for you, everyone is coming in a single day."

Outside the window, a cardinal flitted from the maple tree nearest the house to the big oak along the road. If only she could fly away like that bird. "Fine. One time. Nothing after that."

"And Naomi?" He touched her arm. "Can we move on from this misunderstanding? At least enough to work together?" His voice held a note of pleading.

What choice did they have? Simon expected their help. If they didn't do it, who would? "If you will promise me one more thing."

"What's that?"

"Think before you speak."

"It's never been one of my strong suits but something I'm working on." He tipped his head and gave her a lopsided smile.

At his boyish expression, she almost laughed. Almost. Instead, she sat on the bench at the table, and he joined her.

"What is all this? I expected a folder, not so many papers."

With a shrug, he pulled a folder from the top of the box. "This is what we need for now. Later on, we'll get to what the rest of the box contains. Here's the contract for the auctioneer. Read it over and let me know if you see any problems."

She rubbed her gritty eyes, but the words blurred on the page. And her brain couldn't make sense of the legal wording. After only a minute or so, she handed the papers to Elam. "This is nothing but gibberish to me. If you think it's fine, go ahead and sign it."

"Simon told me it is the same as last year, so I think we'll be okay."

All of the sudden, the world spun, and Naomi grabbed the table to keep from falling over.

Elam dropped the papers. "What's the matter? Is something wrong?"

Nausea accompanied the bout of dizziness. "I don't feel well."

"Let me get you a glass of water." He jumped to his feet and returned in short order. "Here, this should help."

She sipped the cool drink. *"Denki."*

He gathered the papers. "We can finish the rest of this another day. You're quite pale. Maybe you should lie down."

"Nein, I'm fine. We can finish."

"Are you sure? I don't want you to overdo it."

She motioned for him to return to his seat. As he brushed against her on the bench, her arm tingled. He slid away, putting some distance between them, cleared his throat and rummaged in the box. Was he uncomfortable? Did these same feelings that coursed through her make him uneasy, too?

Her mind whirled. "You know what, let's forget about the auction today. I'm too tired to be of much help."

"Then I should leave you to rest."

Nein, for whatever reason, she didn't want him to leave. "I have to feed Joseph in a little while, and then he'll nap, so I can sleep then. There's something I want to show you first."

"Are you sure? I caught your mamm's eye as I came in. She's none too happy about my being here. If I don't let you rest, I'll irritate her even more."

"I'm a grown woman. If I want to show you something before I lie down, then I'll show you something." Was this what a year of widowhood did to her? Made her stand up for herself?

Elam slapped his thighs. "Alright, then, what is it you want to share with me?"

"Come on." She stood and led the way to the door between the main home and the *dawdi haus*, peering over her shoulder to speak to Elam, still not understanding the pull to show him this. Maybe to prove to him she had put the past, including him, behind her and was moving forward. Without him. "Since Grossmammi died two years ago, it's been empty. But it's the perfect solution for me. I can be close to my parents yet live my own life with Joseph."

"Do you really want to be alone?"

The answer was *nein*. She didn't want to live by herself. Then again, she had been a married woman, had run her own home, and she missed that part of her life. "I can't rely on them forever. That's not their job." She turned the doorknob and entered.

The stale odor of cooking oil still hung in the air. There, in the corner of the living room, Grossdaadi had relaxed in his olive-green armchair every evening, the sweet smoke from his pipe curling around his face. And over there, where the kitchen table had once been, Grossmammi had served chicken soup every Saturday evening, the warmth of it filling Naomi's belly.

"Daed has torn out the cabinets. The boxes sagged, and the doors didn't hang right anymore. So many stains colored the ceramic-glazed sink that, unless you knew it had been white at one time, you wouldn't be able to tell."

"A nice, new kitchen will be *gut*." Elam rubbed his flat stomach. "Will you make me a blackberry tart once you move in?"

The reference flooded her brain with memories. "Like we had at Miller's pond the summer before we were supposed to get married?"

"*Ja.* The best I've ever had. Better than my mamm's, though I'd never tell her so."

Naomi chuckled. "The wind blew so hard that day, it knocked your hat off more than once."

"Glad I'm a fast runner, or I would have gone home hatless. What a scandal that would have caused."

"Or you might have had to go for a swim to retrieve it."

"And then I kissed you." Elam leaned closer.

She bent toward him. His lips had tasted like blackberries that day, tart and sweet at the same time. What innocent times those were, when the world was nothing but *wunderbaar*.

Elam pulled her close, so close his breath tickled her neck and shivers coursed up and down her spine. She drew in a deep breath.

And then he backed away. "I'm... I'm sorry. I didn't mean to..." His face reddened until it resembled a ripe tomato.

Her stomach flipped and dipped and did a little dance. He'd been about to kiss her. And she would have let him. He was the one who broke it off. Why?

Never mind the reasons. Kissing him would have been a terrible mistake. She grabbed at her skirt and continued the tour. "The wood floors need to be sanded and stained. In the hall, Grossmammi wore the floorboards almost through as she paced during those long nights while cancer consumed Grossdaadi's body. Once a fresh coat of paint graces the walls, I'll be ready to move in. And start life on my own."

"Why did you show me this?"

"I... Because I remember sitting in the kitchen with you and Grossmammi when you worked for Daed. She always made molasses cookies because they were your favorites. I thought you might like to see the changes."

"Is that really the reason?"

She gestured wide, taking in the entire space. "Because this is going to be my life."

He nodded. "I think I understand." He backed up a step. "Let me know when it's time to install the cabinets. I'd like to help."

"You don't have to." Did she want him here, this close, even for a few days?

"Please, let me do it."

"We'll see when the time comes. I'm sure Daed already has men lined up to lend him a hand." After a last, sweeping gaze, she turned for the porch, clicking the door shut behind her.

"One more thing before I go. There's something in the box I want to show you."

They returned to the kitchen, standing opposite each other, the table between them. The distance she needed to keep herself from becoming overrun with her feelings for him.

He grabbed a plastic grocery bag from the box and pulled out a package wrapped in brown paper. "With Joseph's surgery coming up and all that has happened to you in the past few years, and with how I've messed up everything, I wanted to do something special for you."

Her heart fluttered, but she couldn't decipher what caused the irregular beat. "You didn't need to. I wish you wouldn't have."

"I wanted to." He held out the gift, maybe two feet wide by two feet long and six inches deep.

She unwrapped the paper. Inside was a beautiful wood box. He had dovetailed the corners and stained it a soft golden oak.

Naomi pushed it toward him. "I can't accept it."

Elam's green eyes lost a bit of their luster. "Of course you can. I want you to have it. Things will come up in your life, precious times you're going to want to remember. Mamm tells me children grow so fast. You can put papers in there, maybe little drawings that Joseph will make, or the lock of hair from his first haircut. His first pair of shoes."

She relaxed her shoulders and took it from him. "You did a *gut* job on it."

"*Denki.* My friend Chase let me use his tools. I wanted it to be special for you."

She blinked away the tears that gathered in the corners of her eyes. Why did he get to her like this? He had done a beautiful job. The craftsmanship was superb. He'd been so thoughtful.

"*Denki.* I'll treasure it."

He rubbed her cheek, and her knees went soft. *Nein, nein.* She couldn't allow herself to fall in love with him again.

A light mist obscured the scene outside the van's windows as Frank drove Elam and Naomi to town to order the auction flyers. Yesterday, they had almost kissed, and they shared a tender moment. But he steeled his heart, feelings washing over him. He hadn't quite forgiven her for turning her back on him. And she hadn't forgiven him for leaving. And she never truly might—which meant they had no future together.

Naomi stared out the other window, not saying much.

When they paused at a stop sign, Frank turned. "One more passenger to pick up before we get going. Solomon Mast called last night needing a ride. Something about going to the hardware store for a whetstone to sharpen his lawn mower blades."

Elam choked back the huff that rose from his chest. So far since his return, his childhood friend had avoided him, walking away at church gatherings. Now they would have to share the over twenty-minute ride. Before Elam knew it, Frank pulled into the Masts' driveway, and Solomon climbed into the seat

Naomi had vacated when she moved to the third row.

"Gut morgan." Solomon directed his words to Naomi, giving Elam a brief nod and nothing more.

Elam swallowed hard. "Hello, Solomon."

His once-friend stared straight ahead.

"With the rain we've been having, the grass grows fast, say not?"

And that's what Solomon did. Said nothing.

Naomi leaned forward and whispered in Solomon's ear. He turned to Elam. *"Wie bischt du?"*

"I'm doing fine, *denki*."

Strained silence followed, each second more like an hour. Naomi cleared her throat. "Elam made a very nice memory box for me. And he's crafting picnic tables for the auction."

Solomon harrumphed.

"You're going to have to talk to him sometime."

Naomi's soft words nearly stopped Elam's breathing.

"He broke your heart. Don't be a fool. Elam is like a rabbit. At the first sign of trouble, he scampers away. Can you trust a man like that?"

The question hung on the air.

Elam shifted in his seat. "Don't put her in a position to have to answer such a question. You're not being fair. And I'm through running. I'm here to stay, whether you like it or not."

Solomon now turned to Elam, his red face a contrast to his light hair. "Your actions that night and in the following days hurt more than Aaron and Naomi. You broke the community's trust. And that isn't easy to fix."

Elam swiped a glance at Naomi as her face reddened.

Nein, to put their lives back together would take work. But didn't they see he was trying to do just that? Didn't they see his heart had been broken, too?

No more words were spoken between the car's passengers, and soon enough Frank dropped Solomon at the hardware store and then brought Elam and Naomi to the copy shop. They entered, a chime ringing. No one worked behind the counter.

As they waited for the clerk, Naomi brushed his arm, his breath hitching. "Solomon shouldn't have said what he did. He didn't mean it."

"How do you know?"

"Because I believe you're going to stay."

He spun to face her, her pretty eyes the

Chapter Nine

With each clip-clop of Sugar's hooves on the asphalt, Naomi's stomach clenched tighter and tighter as she neared Elam's home, like clamps were screwing into her midsection. She rubbed her eyes, gritty from lack of sleep last night.

And this was only the practice session for talking to the reporters. What would her nerves be like when the real day came? She couldn't do this, just couldn't. As soon as she arrived, she would tell Elam to call it off. Somehow, the people would come. Somehow, they would earn enough money for the district's needs.

The Yoders' farm came into view, the large, white clapboard house, the green roof and the blue curtains at the windows much like every other Amish home in the area. Dark pants color of periwinkles, her gaze never veering from his face. She truly did. While it wasn't much, it was something. Perhaps the start of the road to forgiveness.

and dresses in an array of colors clung to the clothesline as they snapped in the breeze. A horse whinnied.

She pulled in the driveway and reined Sugar to a stop. Before she could climb from the buggy, Elam sprinted from the house, two fishing poles and a tackle box in his hands. *"Gut morgan."*

What was he up to? "I thought we were going to rehearse what I'm going to say to the reporters next week."

"And so we are. But Mamm is in a cleaning frenzy, and I have a longing to go to Miller's pond. Look at the blue skies. It's the perfect day."

So was the day he took her there and kissed her for the first time, just as dusk settled around them and the frogs took up their nighttime croak. All had been right with the world then. At that moment, she'd believed nothing could ever go wrong.

And then it had.

His shoulders drooped. "This isn't easy for either of us. And I remember what happened there. Don't worry. I have nothing more in mind than catching a few smallmouth bass to fry for dinner. There's no rule that says we have to do all our work at the kitchen table.

Especially not on such a fine day. Can't you smell summer in the air?"

"How can you smell a season?"

"The magnolia tree beside the house is blooming, it rained last night and the earth is plowed. The air is sweet."

"And you're a dreamer."

"Call me what you want. What do you say?"

"Fine. We can practice while we fish." She scooted over and handed him Sugar's reins, her hands shaking.

He touched them. "Are you *narrisch*?"

"Very."

"There's nothing to be afraid of. Pretend you're in your living room speaking to a cousin you haven't seen in a while, telling her about Joseph."

"What if I say something wrong?"

"What could you say wrong when you're sharing with people what has happened in your life? You're worried about nothing. And if they have questions, they'll ask. That's their job."

For the rest of the ride to the pond, Naomi stared straight ahead and clasped her hands in her lap. Of course Elam would reassure her about the meeting. He'd lived among the Englisch for three years. Plenty of time to get to know their ways. She avoided working the front counter at the bakery so she didn't have to speak to them. She hated talking to people she didn't know, and especially in English.

He pulled the buggy from the main road down a wide path and drove deep into the woods, the trees bursting with life, until the pond opened before them, sparkling in the sun. In short order, they baited their hooks, cast them into the water and sat on the dock to watch and wait.

"How are your plans for your new business coming?" She jiggled her pole, attempting to get a fish to bite. Anything to avoid talking about reporters and newspapers.

"Stalled at the moment. Isaac has sold his ranch and will return in the not-too-distant future. With your daed refusing to let me borrow his equipment and his shop, I might have to go back to working construction until I save enough for the tools I need and a place to work." He pulled in his line and fiddled with adding bait, never looking at her.

She caught the downturn of his mouth. "Will you go back to Madison?" Her words floated out in a whisper.

"When I came back, I came back to stay. No matter what people like Solomon say or think about me. They're going to have to put up with me, because I'm not going anywhere. I tried to run from my problems, but they followed me. Better to stay here and deal with them."

"I'm glad to hear that." And she was, no doubt about it. Maybe he had changed. Maybe... *Nein*, better to not let her thoughts get away from her. Once the auction was over, they could go back to being acquaintances, people who ran into each other in the store or at church services. Nothing more. She rubbed the arm that held the pole. "Working for a boss isn't your dream, is it?"

"*Nein*. But I'll have to do just that until I can save my money." His pole bent.

"You have a bite." Naomi bounced on the dock. "Pull it in. See what you got."

"I am, I am." With a chuckle, he reeled up the line until a muddy-green fish popped above the water's surface.

"Oh, that's a nice one." The fish wriggled on the lure.

"A keeper for sure." Elam hooked him to the stringer and plopped the bass into the water. His face shone like he was a six-year-old with his first catch. "I remember how proud Daed was of me the first time I brought home enough fish for everyone for dinner. He complimented me the entire meal. Mamm had to caution him about his boasting and warn me about pride."

At his words, an idea popped into Naomi's mind. She didn't bother to think about it before blurting it out. "Won't your daed let you use a corner of his barn for your shop? That way, you can start your business as soon as Isaac takes over the farm."

"I haven't asked him. Guess I'd just rather be independent. And I'd still need the tools."

"What's the harm in talking to him?"

Elam pushed out a breath. "I don't know if I can."

"Why not?"

"Because he might say no." Elam stared straight ahead, not bothering to cast his line.

Naomi reeled in her hook. "And what if he does? You're no worse off than you are now."

For a moment, Elam was still. Dragonflies flitted over the water. Only the splash of a fish broke the silence. He turned to her, stared at her, his green-eyed gaze going to her lips.

She held her breath.

Then he shook his head and cleared his throat. "I think we'd better go."

And for the second time in as many weeks, her heart shrunk the smallest of bits.

* * *

By the time Elam finished the chores at home and pulled into the Bontragers' place, several other buggies sat in the yard. Through the open kitchen window, the boisterous voices of several men drifted on the breeze. The salty sweetness of frying bacon drew him inside. *"Gut morgan."*

The group glanced up as one then returned to eating their breakfast.

Leroy raised an eyebrow. "Naomi is dressing Joseph. She didn't tell me you were going somewhere today."

He didn't know? "I'm not here to work on the auction but to help with installing the cabinets in the *dawdi haus*. She mentioned it to me, and I'd like to put my skills to use."

"We have a full crew."

The men scraped back their chairs and stood, Solomon among them. "We'll see you over there, Leroy." With one last swig of coffee, he exited with the group.

Joseph's cooing cut the tension in the room. Naomi stepped in, her eyes widening. "You came."

"You said your daed probably had enough men, but you can never have too much help, so I'm here."

"I'm glad." A soft smile graced her face.

The *bobbeli* reached out for Elam, and he took him from her arms.

"If you're here, you're here. Give the *bobbeli* back to his mamm, and let's get to work." Leroy scraped back his chair.

A grin crossed Joseph's face, and Elam matched it. After he mussed the child's hair, he handed him to Naomi and followed her daed to the adjoining house.

Cabinets sat helter-skelter around the kitchen, a set of drawings on top of one detailing where they should go. From his tool belt, Elam produced a screwdriver, and while a couple of other men held the cupboard in place, he secured it to the wall. All the while, his mind raced with Naomi's words. Had his stubborn pride gotten in the way and prevented him from doing what he loved? But his daed had let him know with a few choice words how he felt. As soon as Isaac returned, Elam would be on his own again. Daed wouldn't want him hanging around, working in the barn.

What was it she said? That even if Daed turned him down, he'd be no worse off than he was now. True. How much rejection could one man take, though?

"Hand me that box of screws there." Solomon pointed to a white-and-blue box beside

Elam. He passed the screws, and Solomon grabbed them.

The rest of the morning they worked, no one speaking to Elam other than what was necessary to complete the job. Were all their hearts that hard? If so, what chance did he stand with his daed? Why had he even come today? He wasn't proving anything to them.

Midmorning, Naomi brought coffee and Danish for the men. The two of them stepped onto the porch. "My kitchen is coming together. Now I can picture what it's going to look like."

"You'll have a nice home."

She leaned against the rail and sipped from her mug. "How is it going with the men?"

"Could be better, could be worse." He leaned beside her.

"Have you talked to your daed yet?"

"*Nein.* Not sure I'm going to."

"You convinced me to step out in faith and speak to the reporters. It's your turn to do the same."

Maybe she was right. He'd come this far. If his daed gave his business a temporary home, he could be up and running that much faster. That much sooner until he would be ingrained into the district once more.

The door banged shut behind them, and

Solomon strode across the porch and down the steps before pivoting to stare at Elam. "Quitting so soon?"

He stood and crossed his arms. "Not a chance."

Easy to say. Harder to do.

Chapter Ten

Dark, heavy clouds hung over the tables spread with sandwiches, jars of last year's pickles, gelatin and pies of every imagination. The tempting array made it worth Elam's sore muscles from setting up the tables last night in anticipation of the church service and meal at his family's farm today.

If it didn't rain before he filled his plate.

Across the yard, Naomi chatted with some of the other young mothers as their *kinner* ran in circles around them. After his surgery, when he got older, would Joseph be able to chase the other little ones through the grass?

Elam repressed a sigh.

Aaron came into view, maneuvering his battery-powered wheelchair through the grass. He bumped along and skirted a mud puddle last night's rain left, then pulled alongside the table. He grabbed a plate and piled it high with food. Elam chuckled to himself. He had the typical teenage-boy appetite.

But Aaron didn't wheel himself to join the group of young men setting up the volleyball net in anticipation of this evening's game. Instead, he headed for an unoccupied spot under a large oak at the far edge of the farmyard. With each bump of his wheelchair, the plate on his lap bounced closer to the edge of his knees. Aaron, keeping his sights on the direction he was headed, didn't notice it slipping.

Maybe Elam could catch the dish. He sprinted over, but just as he closed in, the paper plate and its contents spilled to the ground.

Aaron halted as Elam sidled up to him. A muscle jumped in the young man's tight jaw, and he clenched the chair's armrests until his knuckles turned white.

"I tried to catch it."

Aaron turned to Elam with a sigh. "Guess I wasn't paying attention to my plate."

Elam bent down and scraped the sandwich and potato salad from the ground. "What are you doing so far from the action?"

Aaron returned his focus to the field beyond the barn and shrugged. A pain tugged at Elam's midsection. He'd done this to him. Confined him to this wheelchair for the rest of his life. One careless, stupid mistake. A few seconds that changed everyone's lives forever. Solomon was correct. That action impacted so many lives.

Why did he have to do it? Why did he have try to use his cell phone to call for pizza? Acid boiled in his stomach and surged up his throat. He bit back the bile. "I'd think you'd want to be over there cheering for the prettiest girl on the team."

"Like she'd ever have me in this condition. *Nein*, I'll just sit here."

"Why not with your other friends?"

"All they talk about is farming, their jobs and courting. I don't fit in with any of that. I… I haven't milked a cow or driven a plow or asked a girl home from a singing since, well, you know."

Did he ever. Elam plopped onto the ground beside him. "But you have your work with your daed. Not everyone farms these days."

"Like Daed allows me to do anything. Staining. That's it. The one thing he thinks I can handle. But I'm capable of running any of the machines, same as before. And though I may not be able to handle a hay mower, I can milk a cow. He won't see it, though. He coddles me like I'm two, afraid I'll hurt myself." Aaron blew out a breath.

"Then show him he's wrong. Like I said before, you're a *gut* carpenter. Make something for the auction. He'll see that you have a knack for it, and he'll be proud of you."

"I don't know if he'll even let me touch his tools."

If no one was watching, Elam would bang his head against the tree trunk. Then maybe the ripping pain in his soul would go away. Aaron had such potential as a woodworker. While Elam had worked for Leroy, he taught Aaron the basics. His pieces were always precise, well made and beautiful. Elam gulped. "I'm sorry." His words carried on a throaty croak.

Aaron scrunched his brows V, so much like his sister did. "What do you have to be sorry for?"

"Are you kidding? What don't I have to be sorry for?"

"The accident was as much my fault as yours."

"That's not true. I fiddled on my phone. If I hadn't done that, I wouldn't have veered from the road and hit the tree."

"And if I hadn't suggested we get a pizza

on the way home, you wouldn't have been on your phone."

A bead of sweat trickled down Elam's back despite the pleasant spring temperature. "*Nein*, I won't allow you to accept any responsibility. The fault, the guilt, is all mine."

"Don't tear yourself in two. We're both to blame. If I hadn't wanted pizza, if you hadn't made the call, if I'd had my seat belt on... That's too many *ifs*. What's done is done. Much as we would like, we can't change the past."

Aaron had a point. All the wishing, all the blaming in the world didn't change what had happened. Because of him. Was this why Aaron's family could forgive but couldn't forget? Everyday life would be a struggle for him as long as he lived. "That doesn't change the fact that I'm sorry. About everything. That you can't play volleyball. That your daed doesn't trust you in the workshop. That you spilled your lunch. Let me get you another plate." Elam stood and brushed the grass from his pants.

Aaron grabbed him by the wrist. "Please do me one favor?" His voice was a low growl.

"Anything." Even one small thing that could start to atone for his sin.

"Don't treat me like a *bobbeli*. I can get my

own lunch. You wouldn't offer to help me if I had two good legs. Let me do this myself. I'm the one who dropped it."

"That's a deal."

Aaron nodded, his straw hat flopping, spun his chair in a circle and headed in the direction of the much-diminished larder of food before spinning around again. "And Elam, I'll think about what you said. About making a few items for the auction. It's only a maybe."

For Elam, that would have to be enough.

With her *bobbeli* sleeping in his car seat in the Yoders' bedroom, a lightness and an emptiness filled Naomi at the same time. So different not to have him in her arms. What would it be like when he had his surgery? How long before she could hold him?

And what if the worse happened?

Nein, she couldn't dwell on those things. She turned her attention from the group of older women chatting on the porch, a plate on each lap holding a piece of pie. Elam and Aaron huddled near the barn's far corner, just in her view. Then Aaron turned and motored to the lunch table, filling a dish with a pile of food.

Elam stood, a plate in his hand, though he

made no move to eat. He stared at Aaron. What had gone on between them?

She wandered in his direction. The women would talk, and so would everyone else in the district. She stopped. Maybe it was best that she avoid him. Then again, everyone would only assume they were working on the auction. Which is what they were doing. She straightened and continued her trek toward him. "I saw you speaking to my brother."

Elam nodded but didn't turn to face her. "We had an interesting talk."

"Not to be nosy, but what was it about?"

"He told me not to blame myself for the accident. That he was at much at fault as me."

Her brother thought he bore some of the responsibility for his condition?

"But he's not. I took away games with friends and walks with girls."

What should she say? At least his guilt was coming home to rest. As it should. "He's fine at our place, where he can get around, where he doesn't have to face others in the district. But here, at Sunday services and such, he withdraws."

Elam spun on one heel, now mere inches from her, his gaze dark, his breath hot. "I will help him. I don't know what that will look like yet, but I will."

The butterflies in her stomach woke up and performed another dance. She pressed her middle to still them. *Ja*, he was sweet, and he should help Aaron. But organizing an auction to pay the bills wouldn't change Aaron's circumstances.

With a shake of his head, Elam threw off his seriousness. A grin crept across his face. "Are you ready for the newspaper interviews on Friday? We got so busy with fishing the other day, we never practiced."

"*Ach*, I haven't had much time think about them." The butterflies multiplied until there were at least three times as many. "I don't know what to say. What are they going to ask me?"

"I've never been interviewed before, but I imagine they'll invite you to tell them your story. And that's what you should do. Don't worry about being fancy and flowery like the Englisch. Just talk to them. They're people like us."

She gave a half laugh. "Not quite."

"They're not alligators. They won't snap you in their jaws and devour you."

A full laugh bubbled up and spilled out. "I never thought they were."

"*Gut*. They'll do all they can to make you

comfortable. And if they ask a question you don't want to answer, you don't have to."

"*Denki* for offering to stay with me. That will make me less *narrisch*."

"Of course." He raised the plate he'd been holding. "I'd better throw this away. Maybe I'll see you on Tuesday at the bakery. My benches sold out, so I need to make more. At least I own a saw and a screwdriver."

"That's *gut*. I'm glad your business is going well."

"In a way it is, in a way it's not. I have plenty of orders but nowhere to build what people want. For now, I can work outside at the bakery, but when winter comes, or it rains, I need a place inside, and somewhere to store my few hand tools. If my daed won't let me use our barn, I don't know what I'm going to do."

Naomi bit her lip as the kernel of an idea sprouted. He was being kind to her. And she had hurt him when she turned her back on him after the accident. Maybe she could help him.

Chapter Eleven

The loamy smell of just-tilled land filled the spring air as Elam brought Daed an after-dinner cup of coffee on the porch. Mamm had traveled to Montana to help Isaac's wife with the packing and the *kinner* as they prepared to come home, so he and Daed were like two bachelors. *Gut* thing Elam had learned to cook while he'd been away, or the two of them might have starved to death.

Daed's left hand shook as he lifted the mug to his mouth. Even with therapy, he didn't use his right hand for much.

"Are you tired? I can help you into the house."

"If I wanted to go inside, I would do it. Don't need any help getting from one place to the other."

"I was just saying…"

"If I need a hand, I'll ask for it. Fair enough?"

"Fine." Elam nodded and settled into Mamm's rocking chair. Gray and pink dusk descended, and the crickets chirped their nighttime songs. Beside him, Daed sipped his coffee.

"You have something on your mind, son?" Daed slurred his words, but Elam understood him most of the time.

How could he share with him about Naomi when putting two civil words together in a row was difficult for Daed? "It's nothing I want to talk about. Not when I'm the one at fault."

"Again?" Daed's voice was softer than Elam had heard in a long time.

"Still." Maybe he could share what was on his heart. "Whenever I see Aaron, I'm reminded of what I did. No wonder people can't forgive me. Then I do stupid things like blurting out the news about the papers in front of that group of women."

"You gave your answer in your question."

"Huh?"

"You were stupid. You have to be smarter. Think before you act."

"That's been my problem my entire life."

"Ever since you were a little *kind*, you always wanted to do things your own way in your own time."

"Hey. You don't have to agree." Elam chuckled.

"And what about Naomi? How does she feel about telling her story to these newspapers?"

"I'm trying to help her."

"Are you sure?"

"Of course. The bishop never wants to advertise much. A few flyers around town isn't going to bring many people here. But an article in the papers around the state will increase our numbers, our sales and the money we bring in. All to help her and everyone in the district. That includes you. I thought that once I did it, everyone would see how *gut* it was."

"Sounds noble, but make sure it's what she really wants. The story is hers to tell and hers alone."

"I will." Daed was in a *gut* enough mood tonight. This was the most they had spoken in one sitting since Elam had arrived home. Maybe this was the time for him to ask Daed for a favor. "I have a business proposition."

Daed set his coffee cup on the small table beside him and gazed at Elam, his green eyes hooded, the right side of his face drooping from the stroke. "Hope you're not going to ask for a piece of the farm. It's Isaac's. You've made it more than clear over the years that you don't want any part of it. That's a bargain you can't go back on."

"*Nein*, that's not what I'm asking." Elam shivered as the pleasant evening took on a chill. "For a while now, I've wanted to start my own woodworking shop. Both Leroy Bontrager and my friend Chase taught me about the business and how to make finely crafted items. I even have a specialty in mind. Outdoor furniture. Things like picnic tables and porch swings and such."

"Go do whatever you want, then."

Elam leaned closer to his daed. "I don't have a space to work."

"Can't you continue using Chase's garage? We don't have anything fancy around here, and the bishop won't take to putting in electricity anywhere in the district, not for any reason."

A sigh begged to be released, but Elam held it in. "I don't want electricity. My aim is to make furniture the true Amish way. Like Leroy does. With gas-powered tools."

Daed wiggled his bushy left eyebrow. "You don't say. What about the construction job you used to have?"

"It's a fine job, and I know many Amish

men do that kind of work. But if I have any chance at being integrated into the district, I'd like to use traditional tools. And set up business in a corner of the barn to start. Just for a while, until I can afford my own shop."

"How do I know you're going to stay this time?"

Elam drew in a deep breath. "I never planned on leaving. When I bought the truck, I didn't know what I wanted. But I fell in love with Naomi and decided that I wanted to live this life. And then, well, circumstances forced me to walk away. But I'm done running. Ready to own up to what I did."

Daed stroked his beard. "You have been working hard. And helping out. I'll have to think about it."

A throbbing pain banged behind Elam's right eye. "You tell me to prove myself, but how can I do that when you take the opportunity away by refusing to let me use the barn?"

Daed grasped the walker's handles and pulled himself to his feet. "I haven't said no. Just said I'll have to think about it. Now I'm going to bed."

"But what about using the barn?"

"Until I make my final decision, you'll have to work that construction job. You'll need the money for tools, anyway. By the time you have enough saved for them, I'll let you know. That's all I have to say on the matter."

"Did Bishop Zook say why he was coming to visit?" Naomi stood beside her mamm and Laura at their long kitchen counter and rolled out a piecrust.

Mamm measured the ingredients for the strawberry-rhubarb filling, and the tang of it filled the air. "*Nein*, he didn't tell your daed what it was about."

"And he wants all of us here?"

"*Ja*, you, me and Daed." Mamm stirred with great gusto.

Naomi draped the crust over her rolling pin and then laid it in the pie plate. There had to be more to the bishop's visit. "What are you not telling me?"

"Nothing." Mamm's face remained expressionless. She told the truth. "But your daed acted funny. Like he was holding back something. Said I should make a large chicken casserole and set two extra places at the table."

"Is the bishop bringing his wife?"

"I have no idea. Daed wouldn't give me a clue. Laura, do you have the chicken cut up and ready to go?"

"Maybe he's invited Elam to lunch." Laura

dumped the casserole into the dish and placed it in the oven.

Naomi wiped her floury hands on her apron. "Why would he do something like that?"

"To give you two his blessing." Laura tipped her head and grinned at Naomi.

"His blessing? To us? Whatever for?" Now her hands went sweaty. Had Elam gone and done something else impetuous?

"I spotted the two of you the other day on the porch. You were so intent on each other, you never noticed me. And I've seen you together after church on Sundays."

"You spied on us."

Mamm plopped the sweet filling into the crust. "Now, girls, that's quite enough."

"You were in the open. I couldn't avert my eyes."

"We weren't doing anything wrong. He was talking to me."

"Whatever you say." Laura flounced away to set the table.

Naomi sighed and slid the pie plate into the oven.

By the time the casserole and the pie were finished baking, Daed and Aaron had come in from the shed and washed up, and Sam tromped in from the barn. Daed rubbed his hands together. "Smells *wunderbaar* in here.

I have three of the best cooks in the world living under my roof. How much better of a life can a man have?"

Naomi glimpsed out the kitchen window as two buggies rolled to a stop in the drive. One, obviously Bishop Zook. The other… *Nein*, it couldn't be. Laura had only been funning her.

But it was. Elam stepped from the buggy and joined the bishop in making his way to the door.

With hands shaking as she turned the knob, she let them in. "Welcome, Bishop and Elam. Lunch is just about ready."

The bishop ducked as he passed through the narrow, low-roofed back hall into the kitchen, but Naomi stopped Elam from following. "What is this about?"

"I have no idea. The bishop just told me he wanted me to come here today with him for lunch."

"Then I have a pretty *gut* idea."

"You might be wrong." But Elam didn't flash his usual boyish grin. Instead, his tanned cheeks flushed.

"I told you going to the papers was a bad plan, but you keep talking me into it. Why do I ever listen?" She stomped away to join the rest of the family. The group sat and had their silent prayer. In addition to asking for a blessing on the meal, Naomi implored the Lord to keep the bishop from being too upset with them if he was here about the papers.

The potpie, the applesauce, the pickled beets and the fresh bread all made their way around the table. Bishop Zook had his plate full before he cleared his throat to speak. "I'm sure you're wondering why I invited myself and Elam to lunch today."

The bite of chicken Naomi had consumed settled like a lump in her stomach.

Daed nodded. "You're always a welcomed guest in our house, though it's curious why he is here." He glared at Elam.

"How is the *bobbeli*, Naomi?" The bishop forked a piece of carrot.

"Healthy for now. The surgery is scheduled for July."

"So I hear. That's *gut* to know he'll get his heart fixed. If the Lord wills, he'll grow into a fine young man. And of course, the auction is coming soon."

"*Ja*, very fast. With Simon laid up, Elam and I have been working hard on the preparations. I believe Daed has some special pieces he made for it this year, and I've been quilting when Joseph doesn't demand my time."

"I'm looking forward to seeing what you've done, though that's not why I'm here. I've heard some disturbing news. My sister tells me that Elam announced you were planning on sharing your story with the Englisch papers in order to get more people to come to the auction."

Naomi couldn't swallow. "*Ja*, that's true." She studied the food on her plate. Her appetite vanished.

"Bishop, it was my idea." At Elam's pronouncement, the clinking of silverware stopped.

"Why?"

Elam's voice didn't falter. "Because I know the district has a great number of medical needs this year, so many will dip into the account to pay their bills. But we don't advertise. Other auctions in the state do, but not ours. Naomi has a compelling story. If she shares it, we could make sure there is enough money to take care of everyone."

Naomi's heart throbbed in her ears, drowning out all other noise in the house. Not that there was any. She glanced up. The color of Daed's face matched that of the beets on her plate.

A muscle jumped in the bishop's jaw. He scraped his chair back and stood. "There will be no going to the Englisch papers. Is that clear? Word gets out enough. For the rest, we trust the Lord."

Elam also came to his feet. "I want to make sure the district's families have all they need."

Naomi covered her face, pain shooting through her head. She should never have listened to Elam. Why had she allowed him to persuade her to go along with his crazy schemes like he always did?

"And they will. That is my job, and the work of the deacons, not yours. You come back here having learned fancy Englisch ways of doing things. But we don't need computers or the internet or even their newspapers. People know about the auction. They come every year. We have never gone without. Don't you dare cross me, young man. To do so would be to end your relationship with this district forever." The bishop stormed out of the house, his lunch untouched, the screen door banging behind him.

Naomi had never seen him this upset, so angry that he couldn't finish his meal. Elam brought out this side in him.

Daed rose from his chair and marched to Elam, the two of them nose to nose. "Get out of my home." The words exploded from his lips. "And don't you ever come back. You have made the bishop angry with us and have tongues wagging all over the district. How much more do you want to hurt the ones I love?"

Elam stood tall. "If the bishop would just listen to me, he would see that I'm right."

"You would put yourself over the bishop? You know more than him now?"

"Not that I know more than him, but what I'm saying is reasonable. I understand he wants to keep our district from the Englisch ways. But the articles would only bring them to the auction, not into our homes."

"The bishop has made his decision, and that is final." Daed poked Elam in the chest. "Don't involve my daughter in this anymore. If you are so determined to make such a big success of this auction, do it yourself."

"If I have to, I will. But remember that I'm doing this to help, among others, your family." Elam strode from the room.

Naomi rose to follow him. She couldn't let him leave like this.

Chapter Twelve

Elam marched from the Bontrager house, the screen door slapping shut after him. Then it slapped again. He turned, and his breath rushed from his lungs. Naomi had followed him. Why?

"Elam, stop." She, too, was breathless.

"What do you want?" His words came out harsher than he intended.

"I'm… I'm sorry about the bishop and my daed. Going to the papers was a bad idea from the start, and I should have talked you out of it. Then none of this would have happened. But they shouldn't have been so harsh with you."

Did she truly care how he was being treated? He clenched his teeth together and then relaxed them. "Why will no one give me a chance? I know all about forgiving and forgetting. And that forgetting is almost impossible in this situation, but there has to be a way to move on."

"I don't know what to say to you." Her soft, gentle voice touched him deep inside, an ache growing and spreading throughout his body. "Maybe there isn't a way. The damage is done and can't be undone. The wounds are too raw. My family has been through two terrible tragedies in the last three years, and now we're dealing with Joseph. We're just trying to get our feet under us. To figure out life."

"Is my coming back interfering with that?" She was so tiny, so fragile. He forced himself not to reach for her, to hold her as he once had. To comfort her. The hurt in her eyes stirred the tiny seed of love that had lain dormant in his heart.

She shuffled her bare feet in the soft, brown dirt. "That's hard to say."

He stepped toward her until he stood right in front of her. Touched her chin. Forced her to look him in the eyes. "Be honest with me. Tell me what is really deep inside you. Are you still angry with me? Still in love with me?" His heart slammed against his ribs as he held his breath.

"Please don't make me answer those questions. You called it unfair when Solomon asked me." She gazed at him with such intensity, he almost forgot where he was.

"I wish I could help you."

"Is that why you really came back? Did you hear about Daniel and Joseph and figure you had another chance with me?"

"*Nein.* I knew you had married Daniel, but not about his death or Joseph's birth. My parents didn't tell me much about you or your family while I was gone. They only sent me a couple of letters, and not very newsy ones. But I did return in part because of you. And Aaron." They stood face-to-face, inches apart, her breath soft and warm on his neck. "To make up for my mistakes."

"You told me this already. There's no need to go over it again."

"Then tell me if my coming back was worth it."

"The timing wasn't good."

His mouth went dry. Did he dare ask the next question? He swallowed. "Do you want me to leave?"

She pushed away from him. "That is not my decision."

"This is my home, but I'm not welcomed here."

"Did you listen to the bishop? You have always had a mind of your own, done your own thing. The last time, with that truck, it proved to be disastrous. Whatever you do, think it through, and think it through well." Her words weren't harsh but soft and determined. "Remember what the bishop said. If you are going to stay here, you must obey him and submit to the Lord's will." She kissed his cheek, gentle and short, and then returned to the house.

He could do nothing but stand and stare at the spot where she disappeared. Some of what she had said was positive. She hadn't told him to hightail it back to wherever he'd come from. She even pecked him on the cheek. What did that mean? She must have feelings of some kind for him.

Nein, he had to stop these thoughts. He couldn't allow himself to open his heart to her when she hadn't forgiven him. And when her father forbade it.

The bishop didn't approve of Elam's idea of going to the papers. He understood. Once they had opened their district to outsiders. Many came and invaded their lives. Their young people, men like him, left the faith. A few came back. Most never returned. That forced the bishop to restrict their contact with the Englisch as much as feasible.

But in this case, he was wrong. The Englisch didn't want to eat in Amish homes or set up bed-and-breakfasts on their farms. They didn't want to tour the barns or the woodworking shops. They just wanted to come and buy some furniture, some quilts, maybe a tool or two.

From inside came Joseph's little howl, like a sick or wounded dog. Poor thing. He suffered so much. Struggled. A song floated on the air. Naomi singing her son a lullaby.

Sleep, my baby, sleep!
Your daddy's tending the sheep.
Your mommy's taken the cows away.
Won't come home till break of day.
Sleep, my baby, sleep!

Sleep, my baby, sleep!
Your daddy's tending the sheep.
Your mommy's tending the little ones,
Baby sleep as long as he wants.
Sleep, my baby, sleep!

Her sweet, soft voice quieted her *bobbeli's* cries.

And Elam knew what he had to do.

Naomi reined Sugar to a halt near the Yoders' side door. She hadn't intended to stop here, and in fact, didn't really want to be here. The news that she had located a couple of large-capacity ice cream churns could wait. Nothing Elam needed to know right away. But here she was.

From the open living room window, the melody of his mamm's song floated on the late spring air, a familiar tune from the *Ausbund*, the Amish hymnal. The last of the year's tulips drooped their heads, preparing to sleep until next year.

"Don't worry, Daed, I'll get it for you."

"*Nein*, I'll do it myself."

"Sit down. I'll be right back." Elam exited the barn muttering under his breath. He kept his attention on the ground so that he almost walked right into her buggy before he glanced up. "*Ach*, Naomi, you gave me a start. I didn't expect you. Did I forget about something?"

Why did his green eyes hold the power to drive every sensible word from her brain? What had she come for? Oh, *ja*. "The Levi Millers have a large-capacity churn. That gives us three, which should be enough, I hope. What do you think?" And now she blabbered.

"That's *gut*. One less thing on our to-do list. Walk with me to the house. Daed needs another cup of coffee."

A few heartbeats passed before he turned to her. "I'm sorry about the other day. I shouldn't have made it sound like I was placing the responsibility of my future on your shoulders. That wasn't fair of me. Only I can figure it out."

The thing was, she didn't want him to go. If he walked away again, much as she hated to admit it, he would leave a gaping hole in her life. But for whatever reason, she couldn't bring the words to her lips. "What do you want to do?"

"Stay." He halted. "When I returned, it was with the intention of never leaving. But do I have a place here?"

Not trusting her voice, she nodded.

"*Denki.* It's nice to know there are a few people who don't resent my presence. My daed did say he would think about allowing me to use the barn."

"That's progress. Thinking is a *gut* thing, say not?"

"Well, you know how patient of a person I am."

She chuckled. "I remember one winter when we were still in school. Every day after class, you ran to the window to check if it had snowed yet. You didn't miss a single day."

"I had that new sled my daed made for me for my birthday."

"*Ja*, from early October on, you drove us all crazy with your talk of the first big storm."

"What's an eight-year-old boy supposed to do when he has a new sled just waiting for him? That hill behind our house was calling to me."

"And as I remember, it didn't snow until December." She climbed the porch steps.

He followed her. "Not enough to sled, that's right."

"At the right time, your daed will give you his answer."

"When Isaac gets home, he wants me to work construction and earn some money for tools. But if he'd let me use the barn, I can build tables and such with what I have."

"Well, you'll need some cash to buy tools with, so that's not a bad thing."

"I suppose not. Anyway, I'm glad I spoke with him. And I'm glad you encouraged me to do so."

Marcus Herschberger, the eight-year-old boy from the neighboring family, scrambled up the driveway, his shirttail flapping as he sprinted. Naomi chuckled. That *kind* always moved as fast as a flood-swollen creek. Maybe someday that would be Joseph.

"Elam, the postman left this letter for you in our mailbox by mistake. It says it's from—"

"Denki." Elam ripped the envelope from Marcus's hands.

"But my daed said—"

"If you go in the house, my mamm just baked a batch of molasses cookies. But you'd better hurry, because I'm coming right after you, and I'm going to swipe every last one."

"No you won't, 'cause I'm faster than you." Marcus bolted for the house.

"Who is it from?" Naomi tried to peek at the return address on the white envelope.

"No one important." He held it behind his back as his face went pink and then crimson, and he raised his shoulders.

Anyone with halfway decent eyes could see he was hiding something from her. Who could he be corresponding with he didn't want her to know about? *Nein*, he wouldn't. "You'd better not be—"

"Elam, where's that coffee? When you promise a man you'll do him a favor, you'd best do it."

His stiff shoulders relaxed. "I have to get that before he's out here. Come in and grab a few cookies yourself."

"Nein, I have to go." She'd been silly to

stop here in the first place. "Were we going to pick up the flyers on Thursday?"

"I have something going on that day. Friday, I think we said."

She nodded. "That's right. I'll see you Friday morning. And Elam?"

He stopped midstep and turned to her. *"Ja?"*

"Please don't do it."

He spun around and strode across the yard and into the house before she got in the buggy. Her stomach dropped like the thermometer in January. He was up to no good, that much was certain.

Chapter Thirteen

Elam drummed his fingers on the van's door handle as Frank drove him to Madison, rain splatting the windshield and obscuring his view of the greening fields outside the window. If Naomi found out what he was doing today, she'd never speak to him again.

There was only one choice. She could never find out. Not like she almost had the other day when Marcus brought the letter from the Milwaukee paper confirming their appointment. That had been too close a call. As it was, she suspected the truth.

He turned to Frank, the older man leaning forward as he traversed the rain-slicked roads. "Remember, this trip is a big secret. You can't tell anyone in the district what I'm doing."

Frank fingered his graying mustache. "I'll

do my best, but I'm not going to lie. That's where I draw the line."

Though not Amish, Frank was a *gut* and upright man. "I'd never ask that of you. But you don't have to say anything more than that it's a surprise." And if anyone found out about it, it would surely be. "You can tell them you took me to buy a diesel engine. That isn't a lie. I do need to stop at the hardware store." The first piece of equipment he'd need for his shop. If Daed didn't let him store it in the barn, he'd have to keep it in his bedroom.

"Are you sure about this?"

"*Ja*, I am. For Naomi's sake and all the others. I understand the bishop's wish to keep outsiders at arm's length, but this auction is for a single day. A few hours that will benefit many."

"And you're willing to risk your return to the district for this?"

A wave of nausea turned his stomach inside out. Was he? If today's actions became public, at the very least, he stood to earn Naomi's ire forever. She had warned him earlier in the week.

And the bishop's reaction? At the worst, he would drive Elam from the district and bar him from ever returning. Since he hadn't been baptized before he left the first time, he couldn't be shunned. But Bishop Zook would come as close as he could to such an action. He had said so in as many words.

"I've debated the consequences. If I ever expect to experience any kind of forgiveness from the people of this district, if I ever hope to regain any kind of standing, I have to do something to prove to them that I'm sorry for my actions. This is the best way I can think of."

"Going against the bishop will show them you've changed?"

Elam rubbed the back of his neck. "Yes. No. I don't know." His insides churned more. "It will. I'm here to make a difference in people's lives. To better the community."

"Are you sure you aren't doing this for just one reason? To get back in Naomi's good graces?"

Was he? If that was his motivation, then maybe he needed to rethink this strategy. Because if she found out, he had no chance with her. Pictures of a blue-lipped Joseph, a broken-legged Simon, a droopy-mouthed Daed flitted before his eyes.

Nein, his motives were noble. He was doing what he had to in order to help Naomi and the rest of the district. If it took disobeying the bishop, so be it. This was for everyone's benefit.

Frank let him out at the fast-food restaurant just as the rain let up. He went inside and doffed his hat, sitting in a booth overlooking the parking lot. The greasy hamburger and salty fry aroma that permeated the place did nothing to quell the rolling of his stomach.

Maybe he should leave. Maybe Frank was right. This would only bring him more trouble.

But then Frank's white van splashed onto the street and drove away.

The first reporter arrived, a dark-haired woman wearing blue jeans and a long dark shirt. Elam came to his feet as she approached. "Hello."

She flashed him a brilliant white smile and shook his hand. "Thanks so much for agreeing to meet with me." She sat across from him. "Tell me about this little boy."

From there, the story flowed. And it flowed two more times with the other reporters. They each expressed their interest in Joseph's predicament and in promoting the auction. How could this be a bad thing? Especially when the Milwaukee paper promised prominent coverage for it in the Sunday edition.

Once the last journalist left, he repositioned

his hat on his head and walked from the restaurant. The cool rain-washed air filled his lungs. Despite what the bishop said, what he'd done here today wasn't a bad thing. Quite the opposite. So much *gut* would come from the Englisch learning the Amish were no different from them in many ways. They faced much the same struggles. They worked to keep their families strong and healthy.

As long as no one in the district found out, things would be fine.

With the sweet perfumes of sugar and cinnamon clinging to her clothes, Naomi hurried from the bakery's kitchen, through the enclosed breezeway, and to the Herschbergers' door. *Gut* thing she didn't have to dash through the rain to get here. Water dripped from eaves. What a gloomy day.

But her mission here might turn the day into a nice one.

After a few moments, Sylvia answered her knock. "Well, Naomi, what a pleasant surprise. Come in and let me put the coffeepot on. What a chilly day. Almost like fall, say not?"

"*Denki*, but I don't need any. After several hours beside the ovens, I'm plenty warm. Is Simon around?"

"I'm here. Not like I can go many places these days." He rolled his wheelchair in from the living room.

"And as pleasant as always." Sylvia harrumphed, but her eyes twinkled. So did Simon's.

Naomi chuckled. "I'm glad you're in a fine mood, because I've come here for a favor." She rubbed the end of her prayer *kapp* string. Silly that she should hesitate in asking.

"Sit down." Sylvia pulled out a chair and motioned for Naomi to have a seat. "You know you can ask us anything."

Why did her stomach do such somersaults and flips? Simon and Sylvia were *gut* friends. They were among the few who embraced Elam when he returned. She drew in a deep breath. "Simon, you assigned me and Elam to work on the auction together." She studied her sturdy black shoes. "I have to admit, I wasn't very happy about it at first."

She glanced up as Simon stroked his beard. "I know you weren't. I saw the hardness in your eyes when you looked at him, how you walked away whenever he came close. But the Lord, in His providence, brought the two of you together when I fell. I couldn't resist. Have you had problems?"

"*Nein.* Not really. A few bumps along the

way, but everything is going well now. And since the bishop forbade us from speaking to the papers, that's one less item for me to worry about." Maybe.

"*Gut*, that's very *gut*." Simon nodded.

Sylvia came to the table with the coffee-pot and, not taking no for an answer, poured Naomi a cup. Then she sat down and glared at her husband. "You didn't break your leg on purpose, did you, just to get these two together? I thought scheming and matchmaking were a woman's domain."

"You give me too much credit. I just saw an opportunity and took it."

With a smile pasted onto her face, Naomi sat back and sipped the black brew. Oh, to have a marriage like that, a home with fun and laughter, a man and a woman who loved each other in such a way. Joseph squealing in glee as his daed tickled him and threw him in the air. Her little boy curled up between them in the evenings as they read the Bible.

"Naomi? Naomi." Sylvia patted her hand and thrust her into reality. "I think you were woolgathering."

"Oh, I'm sorry." She squirmed under their scrutiny.

"What has brought you here?"

"You've already been so kind to me and Elam, but I'd like to ask another favor."

"Nonsense." Simon waved her away. "I owe you a great debt for stepping in the way you have. Both of you."

"Elam wants to open a shop that builds outdoor furniture, like the picnic tables he makes for you."

"And such a fine job he does, too. The Englisch can't buy them fast enough. He'll do well." Simon repositioned himself in his wheelchair.

She couldn't get the picture of Aaron out of her mind. Of his struggling with everyday tasks. She cleared her throat. "He needs a place to run his shop. His daed won't let him use his barn, at least not right now, and mine won't allow him to work in our shop. You have that big barn and—"

"I have the buggy horse in there and not much else. With a little rearranging, there should be plenty of room for him to work."

"Denki, denki, denki." Naomi clapped her hands. "He's spoken of getting a place of his own once the business is going, but this will give him a start. And don't say a word to him. I want to be the one to tell him."

"He won't hear it from me." Simon peered at his wife.

"And not from me either."

"He'll be so grateful, I have no doubt. How can I ever repay you?"

Simon crossed his arms and narrowed his eyes. "If I hear one more word about it, the deal is off. You just concentrate on the auction and on getting your son well."

With a lightness in her step, Naomi restrained herself from skipping to her buggy. The rain had even stopped. As she went to retrieve Sugar from where she grazed, Elam pulled in and unhitched Prancer. "Just getting off work?"

Heat grazed her cheeks, and her mouth went dry. He grinned like a little *kind*, and her heart stopped for a moment. "A little while ago."

"Hmm, sounds mysterious."

"Mysterious? Ah, *nein*, not at all." She scuffed her shoe in the mud. "Just had a little chat with Sylvia and Simon."

"You take care of yourself. I see how tired you are. The auction will be over soon, and then the surgery. I don't want you to get sick." Then the softness in his face disappeared, and he stepped back.

"I will. You, too."

He strode toward the house, and she grasped her chest in an effort to slow her pounding heart.

She would have to find a very special way to tell him her news.

Chapter Fourteen

A bead of sweat rolled down Naomi's back and between her shoulder blades. Joseph slept in his car seat under the shade of the tree. Almost everything was in place for tomorrow. The big auction. The ladies who helped her set up the quilts in the auction building had left. She turned to Elam who had come earlier to lend a hand and go over the last of the preparations. "That should just about do it until the men arrive with the tents and the truck comes from the greenhouse with the plants." She checked on her *bobbeli*, his downy head damp with perspiration.

Elam perused the grounds. "They should be here soon." He wiped a trickle of sweat from his jawline. "If it's this hot tomorrow, the ice cream will be the most popular food item."

"I'm glad it's almost over."

He sat on the lawn beside Joseph. "Why?"

"Mostly because the work will be done. We'll know how much money we have, and Joseph can have his surgery." She studied her son, his lips tinged blue, his arms and legs scrawny, all because of his heart condition.

He touched her hand, and she didn't pull away. A strength flowed from him, a surety that stilled the frantic pounding of her heart when she gazed at Joseph. "It will be fine. You'll see. He'll grow into a strapping young man."

"But what if he doesn't?" She turned to him, his eyes not twinkling with his usual mischievous gleam. "What if I lose my son?"

"Worry ends where faith begins. That's what Mamm always says."

She stroked Joseph's pale cheek. "I want to move time forward, so that the operation will be over, and he'll be fine. But I want to stop the clock's hands and keep him safe here, in this moment."

"That's understandable. You love him. I'll pray for him. And for you. I always do."

She couldn't so much as glance at Elam, or she'd cry. No way would she be able to tell him about the surprise right now.

Another buggy pulled into the lot. Sylvia steered the horse toward where they were.

In the back, Simon sat with his casted leg on a pillow.

Elam helped Naomi to her feet and led her by the hand to the Herschbergers. "You're looking well, Simon."

The old man nodded. "And everything here is in order?"

Elam grinned. "It's coming together."

"Seems to me the two of you did well." Simon repositioned himself in the buggy. "Hopefully we'll have a good turnout, and the auction will be a resounding success. I knew when I put you both in charge of this you would pull it off just fine."

"I'm expecting a big crowd." Elam almost bounced on his toes. The glimmer returned to his green eyes. He was up to something. She knew him too well. Underneath his hat, he hid a secret.

Did she really want to know what it was?

Simon leaned against the back of the buggy. "Alright then, put me to work. Tell me what I should do so I don't feel like a broken wheel."

Elam chuckled, rich and deep like the spring's first maple syrup. One of the things about him she'd first fallen in love with. "You have the most important job of all, because you get to tell us what to do." He laughed again, and Simon joined in the merriment.

She turned away. Elam was a charmer, no doubt. And his charm had melted some of the ice around her heart. She steeled herself against the rising tide of feelings.

With the men here now to complete the heavy work, she collected Joseph from under the tree. Time to go home and help Mamm get dinner on the table. As she settled the car seat in the buggy, she glanced up. Aaron drove into the lot.

He waved her over. "I have a delivery here. Could you give me a hand?"

"I only have a few minutes. Joseph will want to eat soon." She peered into the back, loaded with any number of sweet wooden toy trains and three large dollhouses. "You made these?"

He nodded so hard his hat flopped on his head. "Sure did. I wanted to do my part. That's where I've been spending my evenings this past week and why I've been going to the shop early."

"They're beautiful." She picked up a train and reveled in the smoothness of it, as silky as rabbit's fur. "I'm going to have to buy one for Joseph. When he learns to walk, he'll love to pull one of these around."

"Don't worry. I have one set aside for him. No charge."

Elam strode to the buggy, whistling, his hands in his pockets as if he didn't have a care in the world. He, too, examined Aaron's craftsmanship. "They'll sell fast. You're turning into a fine carpenter."

"*Denki* for motivating me to do this, to do more than I thought I could. Certainly more than Daed thought I could."

Naomi tipped her head and stared at Elam. He had done that for her brother?

Before the sun had risen very high in the sky, Mamm pulled the buggy to a stop at the edge of the auction grounds, and Naomi scanned what the men had accomplished after she'd left yesterday. A smattering of people, a mix of Amish and Englisch, milled around the building where the quilt and furniture auction would take place. Off to the side, the men had pitched a large white tent in the grass, home to the woodcrafts and garden goods sale. Later, on the other side of the building, the tool and farm implement auction would take place. Nearby, Daed sat with the ice cream churns, waiting for the heat of the day to bolster business. And the way the sun blazed already in the cloud-free sky, they would reap a great profit.

"Sam, don't run off on me. I need help

with these pies." Mamm slid from the buggy and pulled apple, peach, strawberry, lemon, cherry, oatmeal and rhubarb pies from the back.

Naomi shifted Joseph on her hip. "Hand me a few of them, and I'll get them to the bakery table."

Mamm gave her a couple to carry.

Laura emerged from the back of the buggy, loaded down with every variety. "I think that's about all. I don't care if I never see another pastry crust in my entire life."

Naomi nudged her. "You will when we have them sliced and ready to sell."

"I didn't say I would never eat another one. I just don't want to look at them." With a giggle, Laura trotted off with the bakery goods.

"*Ach*, will that girl ever grow up?"

"She's just Laura." Naomi followed Mamm to the table loaded with turnovers, doughnuts, pretzels and, of course, the plethora of pies they brought.

By the time they had everything set up and organized and the Millers came to man the table, many more Englisch had arrived, parking their cars, trucks and vans along the narrow country road, walking to the auction grounds and crowding in to ogle everything for sale.

"Isn't it a beautiful day? *Gut* thing it's not raining."

Naomi jumped a mile and almost dropped Joseph in the process. "Elam Yoder, you have to stop scaring people."

With a grin stretched across his face, he showed no signs of remorse. "Think about all we'll sell today and the money we'll raise."

Sylvia wheeled Simon over, his leg propped on pillows, bobbing his head as he took in the scene. "Not to turn either one of you vain or proud, but you've done a *gut* job with arranging the day. Seems to me the items and the sellers are in place and that the sale is running without any hiccups so far. I have to hand it to you. You might just have put me out of a job."

"Naomi, maybe, but not me. This is my one and only time to do this."

Simon frowned. "So, you didn't enjoy it, then?"

"*Nein*, it's not that. But it's best left to others. Naomi did most of the organizing, anyway. I was just the muscle power." Elam pursed his lips.

She tamped down the warmth attempting to rise in her chest, lest she get too prideful. "We worked together well, Elam. I'm surprised to say I enjoyed it. Everyone can see your effort and what a fine job you did."

"*Denki.* That means so much coming from you. Maybe…" He touched her shoulder, then jerked away, his eyes a darker green than ever.

Her breath caught her in throat, and she swallowed. "See, we didn't have to go to the papers. Word got around despite our lack of advertising, and there are plenty of people here. More than I remember in recent years."

Simon nodded. "I've never seen this place so full. Who needs that fancy internet stuff when word of mouth works so well? If you sell quality goods for a *gut* price, then you don't need much publicity. News gets around."

Elam squirmed. Like he was uncomfortable. Or guilty.

"Simon, can you excuse us? I'd like to show Naomi something."

"What are you up to?" She tipped her head and chuckled.

"Come inside the building with me."

She followed him to the large pole barn, her eyes taking a moment to adjust to the dimness inside it after the bright sunshine. Furniture and quilts crammed the front of the building around the platform where the auctioneer would sell the merchandise. Chairs for the bidders occupied the rest of the space. Interested folks browsed the offerings. Everything was just as they had left it last night. "What is it?"

He led her to a row of three Adirondack chairs, the cuts precise. She sat in one, slid back into the depths of it and caressed the armrest. Sanded to a perfect smoothness and stained a lovely honey color. "These are beautiful."

"I'm hoping that between the picnic tables and these, I'll be able to get my carpentry shop going sooner rather than later."

Perhaps this is what he'd been hiding. She shouldn't have been so suspicious of him. She opened her mouth to reveal her surprise, but different words squeaked out. "You donated them to the auction?"

"I would do anything for you and Joseph. For your entire family." He stared right at her, not blinking, his gaze soft. When he did that, she almost believed the words he said. Almost forgot what happened between them.

She broke eye contact with him. "I want to peek at the quilts. Mamm and her friends were working on one, but I haven't seen it since it was finished." She strode away. Elam's footfalls followed her.

To keep from having to look at him or speak to him, she busied herself walking among the rows. Maybe the green Double

Wedding Ring would pay for medication for Joseph. Or the red Star of Bethlehem might bring enough money for a couple of therapy sessions for Aaron. Or this Log Cabin one might be enough to satisfy a doctor's fee for Simon or Elam's daed.

Several Englisch ladies, their arms and legs bare, their sunglasses stuck in their hair, wandered among the quilts, as well. They oohed and aahed over each of them. "I might have to bid on this one." A heavier-set middle-aged woman stroked the blue Center Diamond quilt. "It's beautiful, don't you think so, Tammy? I know Bill will be upset with the amount of money I spend on it, but I have to have it."

"Gina, I won't tell if you won't." The women laughed.

Naomi turned to walk away, but Joseph grabbed for the quilt and hung on with all his might. "*Nein*, little one, you have to let go." She spoke to him in *Deitsch* while loosening his fingers from around the fabric. She glanced up.

The woman named Gina stared at her. "Is that your baby?"

"Yes." If only Joseph would let go. For one so sick, he had a powerful grip.

"You're the lady I read about in the paper.

The one with the child who needs surgery." Gina turned to her friends. "That's why they're having this auction."

Naomi's knees went weak, and her mouth dried out. "You read about me in the paper?"

"Yes. It was a wonderful article about how this helps your people to get medical care. I have a grandson who needed surgery when he was little, and the story moved me so much, I had to come and support you. And look, I brought a bunch of my friends with me. What a good cause. I hope your little boy is feeling better soon."

Naomi turned to find Elam and almost ran right into him. "What have you done?"

Chapter Fifteen

With Naomi staring at Elam the way she did, her eyes wide, her jaw clenched, his stomach tumbled like a rock down a hill. Joseph whimpered as she squeezed him. "I can't believe you went behind my back like this," she hissed.

The Englisch women stared at them. The last thing Naomi and Elam needed was to make a scene in front of the customers. "Please, let's go talk in private. I can explain."

She marched out of the building, and he followed like an obedient puppy. This is what he'd been afraid of. The exact reaction he expected if she found out. How could he have ever thought he could keep it from her?

She led him from the commotion of the auction to a field behind the building, out of earshot of the crowd. "Nothing you say can excuse what you did."

"*Ja*, I went to the papers."

"When the bishop expressly forbade it? Didn't you think? Don't you ever think?"

"I thought I was doing a *gut* thing for you, for Joseph, Aaron, Daed, Simon. So many others."

"Apparently not. Joseph sticks out in a crowd. Everyone will know he is the *bobbeli* from the story. They will stare at us. I can't stand that, being a monkey in a show. I won't have it." Her voice cracked.

He lifted his hat and pulled out a slip of paper and handed it to her. "This is the article. Read it. Please. Then you will know I only did it for your good, for Joseph's, to help you out."

"Now you read the Englisch newspapers?"

"Please, Naomi, try to understand." He walked in a tight circle before facing her again. "No one here accepts me. They treat me as if I'm a criminal. Forgiven, *ja*, but still an outcast."

"So you're doing this to win favor with the district?"

"*Nein*, because I want to help you."

"This will never make up for paralyzing

my brother and breaking my heart." Her breaths came in rapid succession.

His shoulders sagged. "I know. But I love you. That's what I want to prove. That I'm now worthy of that love."

"You're trying to earn it."

"Maybe."

"This wasn't the way. I never wanted anything to do with this in the first place." She crumpled the newsprint and threw it into the long grass. "You've betrayed me. Worse now than when you walked away. Please, I beg you, just leave me alone. All you end up doing is hurting me." A sob escaped her throat, and she ran toward the row of parked buggies, Joseph bouncing on her hip.

Elam stood in the field as the sun beat down on him. Despite the warmth of the rays on his shoulders and his head, he shivered. Didn't the ends justify the means? Maybe he would never win her favor. Or that of the district.

A grasshopper jumped on his shoe, sat for moment and then hopped away. It bounced above the grasses several times before it disappeared. Oh, to have the life of a grasshopper. To be so carefree as to jump everywhere you went, not worrying what people thought about you. Then again, what a solitary life.

He rubbed his temples and pivoted. Simon approached, Sylvia wheeling his chair across the grass. He waved for them to stop and hurried to them.

Simon peered over his shoulder at his wife. "*Denki.* Elam can bring me back," she whispered in his ear, and he smiled as she ambled away. "Now, Elam Yoder, let's talk about you. What are you doing here by yourself? You're missing the fun."

"I'm in no mood for fun."

"Of course you are. You always are."

"Not this time."

"What happened? I saw Naomi run off. That's why I had Sylvia bring me over here. Did you two have a spat? I thought you were getting along well."

"We were, but I did something stupid."

Simon gazed at the intense blue sky. "Are you going to share what it was?"

Elam closed his eyes, not able to look at the man who had been like a grossdaadi to him. "I went to the papers and shared Naomi's story. Without her permission."

"And I heard tell that Bishop Zook forbade you from speaking with them."

"*Ja.*" Elam opened his eyes.

Simon shook his head, just twice. "I love you like you were one of my own family, but

Elam, you sabotage yourself every chance you get." Simon broke eye contact.

An emptiness swept over Elam's midsection. "I know, I know. Why can't I stop myself? I think I'm doing good for someone, and things manage to go awry."

"You don't learn your lessons. You've always been headstrong and independent, going about life your own way. Like I did, back years ago when I was a young man." Simon wiped his sweaty brow with a handkerchief. "Doing what Naomi asks you not to isn't going to win her favor. And going against the bishop's orders might keep you from joining the church and being accepted in the district."

"I know. How could I have been such a *dummkopf*?"

"Or did you hope no one would find out?"

Elam sighed and toed the ground. "Maybe. *Ja*."

"You can never cover your sins."

"So I just learned."

"You should have found that out long ago. But for some of us, me included, we have to learn our lessons the hard way."

"I think I still love her."

"And that's why you did what you did."

"*Ja*. You understand. Why doesn't she?"

"You knew she wouldn't like it. That's why you didn't tell her."

Simon was insightful, no doubt. He never let Elam get away with anything. "And why I didn't want her to ever find out. Because I wanted to help her, not hurt her."

"It's time for you to start getting smart. Woo her the right way."

"But now I have to make up for this and for injuring her brother and for breaking her heart."

Simon gave a single chuckle. "Sounds like you have a lot of work to do."

"That's the problem. I don't know how to go about it."

"Are you ready to listen and take advice?"

"What can it hurt? I can't make things worse than they are."

"That's not true." More cars roared down the street, and a few people wandered along the road to their vehicles, large wooden welcome signs and shovels painted with bright flowers filling their hands. "I know you're a *gut* man. Who else could I have entrusted the auction to? You're a hard worker. But instead of insisting on going about things your own way, think about what others need."

"That's what I did. The church's medical fund needs money for Daniel's care and Joseph's surgery, your hospital stay, my daed's therapy, among many other things. I went to the papers so many Englisch would come today."

"Fine. Point taken. Not what others need. What they want."

Elam scratched his chin. What people wanted, not necessarily what they needed? That was a new way of looking at life. "You might be right. I've been trying to win over Naomi the wrong way. And everyone else in the district." Now all he had to do was to find out what Naomi wanted and give it to her.

But what she'd said when she ran off was for him to leave her alone.

He wasn't sure he could give her that.

Naomi's heart pounded against her chest and throbbed in her ears as she sprinted across the auction grounds to the line of buggies. She scrambled inside her family's and slumped against the sun-warmed seat. She cradled Joseph to herself and cried.

"Why, oh why would he do something like that? Can't he leave well enough alone? He's come back here, Joseph, and turned our lives upside down. As if they weren't already in disarray. What am I supposed to do?"

She sat against the seat and sobbed until

sweat mingled with her tears. But she couldn't go back there. Couldn't show her face around here today. People would stare at her. Already, the weight of their gazes bore down on her. She had promised to work the bakery table for a while, but she wouldn't. Couldn't. They would make out fine without her.

Nausea rolled through her midsection, and she fought to keep her breakfast inside. Joseph fussed, probably hot and hungry. "Hush, my *bobbeli*, we'll find a way to let Mamm and the others know we need to leave. We just have to do it without being seen."

"There you are."

Naomi sucked in a lungful of air, adrenaline flooding her arms and legs. "Rachel. I didn't see you coming."

Her dark-haired friend climbed aboard and sat beside her. "Sorry. I tried to make some noise, but you must have been too deep in thought."

Naomi turned toward her friend.

She touched Naomi's arm. "*Nein*, not too deep in thought. Your eyes are red and puffy. You've been crying. What's wrong?"

"Elam. The auction. Joseph. Everything."

"Elam. I should have figured he was the source of your tears. What has he done now?"

"Remember I told you about his ridiculous scheme to go to the papers?"

"*Ja*, the one the bishop put a stop to."

"Well, you know that Elam isn't always the best at listening."

"That's an understatement. But don't tell me. He spoke to them anyway. Did you know about this?"

"Of course not. After Bishop Zook's visit, I told him to forget the idea, that it wasn't a *gut* one in the first place. I never spoke a word to them. But of course, he did his own thing and apparently granted the interviews on my behalf."

"Sounds like Elam."

"And if I go out there now, everyone will stare at me and Joseph. They will feel nothing but pity for us. I don't want that. Can't life go back to normal?"

Rachel handed Naomi a handkerchief, took Joseph from her and jiggled him on her knee. "I hate to tell you, but this is normal life. Elam is back, and it seems he's not going to leave. You're going to have to figure out a way to live in the same district together."

"That would be fine if he wouldn't come around me."

"Tell me, Naomi, what is in your heart?

You wouldn't be this upset about Elam if you didn't feel something for him."

"That's what I mean when I say nothing is normal. I once loved Elam. Very much."

"And he broke your heart."

"So I married Daniel. *Nein*, it wasn't the crazy kind of love like Elam and I had. But Daniel was *gut* to me. Took care of me. In a different sort of way, I loved him. And then God took him away from me and left me with a son to raise."

"Does Elam still stir those feelings in you?"

"He shouldn't."

Rachel tucked a damp strand of stray hair under her *kapp*. "That's not what I asked."

The problem was, he did. But it wasn't good. Elam brought nothing but disaster to her family. It would be best if he kept his distance from now on. "I won't let him hurt me again."

"What are you going to do about it, then?"

"Avoid him as much as possible." Naomi grabbed Rachel by the hand. "Which means I need you to stay right beside me all the time. At the bakery and at service. You can talk to him so I don't have to."

"You're going to run into him at times when I'm not around."

"Then I'll find a way to be somewhere else, somewhere he can't come. In the kitchen. In my bedroom."

"In this buggy." Rachel laughed, and Joseph mimicked her. "*Ja*, that was funny, wasn't it, *bobbeli*? You tell your mamm that everything will work out fine in the end."

Naomi kissed her son's round cheek. "We are very blessed to have Rachel for such a *gut* friend. And you will have your operation, your lips won't be blue, and things will settle down once more. We will be happy, you and me, my precious son. I will make it so."

Rachel squeezed her hand. "That's what I like to hear. God will give you strength for each day. Elam will learn you don't care for him anymore and will go away. Perhaps another fine young man will capture your heart."

"I can't think about that, but *denki*, Rachel."

"Let me get my horse, hitch him to my buggy and take you home."

"And tell my mamm. Not why we're leaving, just that we're going. Say I have a headache, which is the truth. I'll explain to my parents once we're at the house."

Rachel left to get her horse, and Naomi

eased against the back of the seat. Through the little back window, she had a view of the Englisch coming and going. Some left with nothing more than a doughnut in their hands, while others walked away with wooden garden sculptures and flats of petunias. The quilt and furniture auction hadn't yet begun.

When Joseph cried, she turned her attention to him, wiping the sweat from his broad forehead as he breathed his raspy breaths. "Just a couple more weeks, little one, and you won't struggle so much. You'll feel better and can grow big and strong."

"Naomi."

The soft voice didn't startle her. But it set her hands to shaking. Elam. And, of course, Rachel hadn't returned yet. "I don't want to talk to you."

He came around the side of the buggy. "I'm not asking you to. All I wanted to say is I'm sorry. Not just because you found out about what I did, but because I went against your wishes and the bishop's, and I hurt you again. That's the last thing I wanted. And so, I apologize. Whether you accept it or not, please know it's sincere. And now, I won't bother you anymore."

Long after the crunch of his shoes on the

gravel faded away, Naomi sat in the buggy and stared straight ahead. He'd agreed to her terms. Even so, a little part of her went with him.

Chapter Sixteen

✑

"Just a little over a month until Joseph's surgery, right?" Rachel strolled beside Naomi as they searched for a spot in the Millers' yard after Sunday service to sit and have their lunch.

"*Ja.* And I'm getting nervous." The smell of meal, the tang of the pickles, the sweetness of the strawberries, which had set her stomach to rumbling just a few minutes ago, now set it to churning.

"He'll be fine. You told me the doctors are very good. They have done this surgery many times, so you have nothing to worry about."

"They also say there is always a risk with the operation."

"Of course they do. They're supposed to tell you that. But he's young. Babies are resilient. That's what Mamm says. They can be so sick and bounce right back."

The doctors had told her all this. But while her head knew the risks were small, her heart trembled. "He's so little. And not very strong." She stroked her boy's bony hand.

As they meandered around the yard, dodging *kinner* racing through the grass, Rachel leaned over, nose to nose with Joseph. "*Ach*, tell your mamm that you're bigger and stronger than you look. In a few months, you'll be getting around, and she won't be able to keep up with you. She'll wish for a little peace and quiet then."

Naomi pointed to the house, the one that had been Daniel's before they married, so familiar to her. "How about the porch step? That's a *gut* place, and it's in the shade right now."

"Fine with me. I can't believe how hot it is for June in Wisconsin. I'll be a puddle in another minute if we don't get out of the sun."

The two of them settled on the step. Naomi laid Joseph on a blanket in the grass beside her feet, and he cooed as he stared at the leaves of the maple tree blowing in the slight, very welcome breeze.

"How long will he be in the hospital?"

"That depends on how well he does after surgery. Maybe even less than a week."

"How amazing."

"But I don't know how long I'll be out of work from the bakery. For sure I won't come back until Joseph is fully healed, *gut* and strong again."

"I'm surprised Elam didn't show up at the bakery to pester you this week. He comes in often enough."

"So far, he's been keeping his word about leaving me alone. I haven't seen him at all since last Saturday. Maybe I finally got through to him." She sighed. *Ja*, maybe she had finally gotten what she wanted.

"You don't sound happy."

"I don't know what I feel anymore. Part of me was disappointed when he didn't come by. But it's for the best that he stays away. He only complicates my life."

"Who does?" Aaron maneuvered his chair up the walk to where they sat.

"Elam."

"You've been sulking for over a week."

"Shouldn't I be? He went and told my story behind my back, and without the bishop's permission. How else am I supposed to act?"

"I don't know. Maybe he shouldn't have

done it, but did you think about why he spoke to the reporters?"

"Because I wasn't going to cross the bishop."

"*Nein*, because he wanted to help you. And me. And everyone else. That's all. Sure, he doesn't always make the best decisions, but he always has the good of others in mind."

"That doesn't make it right." This was a battle she'd fought inside herself all week. Did his intentions make a difference in what he did? Did they make his actions acceptable? Or at least good? "But what about you?"

Aaron furrowed his light eyebrows. "What about me?"

"He may have had *gut* intentions, driving that night while ordering pizza for you, but that doesn't justify what happened. He caused the accident that paralyzed you. Others end up paying the consequences for his poor choices." She glanced at Joseph, who sucked on his bare toes.

"The accident happened because I asked him to call ahead and order."

"That's not an excuse. He was older. The one who should have known better."

Aaron leaned forward. "I don't blame him."

That is what Elam had told her. "You don't blame yourself, do you?"

"Sometimes, maybe. But I know it wasn't all Elam's fault. And he shouldn't have to pay the rest of his life for one mistake."

"You have to."

Aaron shook his head. "It's not what I would have chosen for myself, but it is what it is. I have to deal with it. You can't punish Elam. Even the state of Wisconsin only gave him a fine for distracted driving. If I were you, I'd think about the good he's done. He's trying. You have to give him credit."

"If that were true, wouldn't you be joining in with the others in your age group instead of hanging back?"

"Well…"

"You should, you know. Look, you went and made those trains. You proved to yourself you could do it."

"*Ja*, I suppose I did."

"Then you can do this. They're starting a volleyball game. Go over there. Maybe you can serve."

Aaron stared in that direction for a long moment, then sat up straight and rolled away, bumping over the uneven ground toward the group of young people.

And Elam had done this. Encouraged Aaron to start living life. Naomi set her plate aside. "I'm like a stirred pot. All mixed up."

And then Elam rounded the corner of the house. Not the person she wanted to see right now.

He marched up the path and stood in front of them. "Hello, Rachel. Naomi, I, well I've been thinking about you." He shuffled his feet, stuffed inside black shoes.

A chill raced through her. "Please, Elam."

"I know I said I'd stay away, and I will. But I have to say again that I'm sorry I hurt you. With God's help, I'll do better. I know you've already given me a second chance, and probably more than that. But I'm hoping I'm similar to a cat. You know, nine lives, nine chances."

She couldn't help but chuckle at his attempt to lighten the mood.

"I can still make you laugh. That is all I've ever wanted to do for you."

A large older man stomped in their direction, his jaw clenched, his eyes narrowed. Bishop Zook. She stood and smoothed her dark blue skirt. "Elam, the bishop is coming this way."

At Naomi's words, Elam's legs lost all strength. He leaned against the porch post for support. Of course the man would have words with him. It was surprising the bishop hadn't tracked him down on the day of the auction. "I haven't seen him since—"

"Elam Yoder. Just the man I was hoping to run into today."

Elam plastered a smile to his face and spun toward the bishop. "Well, you found me."

"Word has gotten around that the turnout at the auction was so large because an article appeared in the Englisch papers around the state about Naomi. And that you were the one who told her story."

His tongue stuck to the roof of his mouth, and he swallowed hard before speaking. "I did. She had nothing to do with it whatsoever."

"Did I tell you that you were not to speak to any reporters? To respect our ways?"

"You did. And I'm sorry for disobeying." His heart pounded like a hammer on his ribs. What punishment would the bishop mete out?

"Or are you sorry you got caught? You had no twinge of conscience when you did this, obviously, or you would have kept your mouth shut. Once we tried opening up to the Englisch more, but that didn't work. I've striven to keep our district as closed as possible. Things are changing, so there must be some contact, but not to this extent. Not when you put one of our young women on public display." A bead of sweat trickled down the bishop's round, reddened face.

"You're right, I shouldn't have done it. When I spoke to them, I wasn't thinking." He bit the inside of his lip. "*Nein*, that isn't true. I was thinking. Thinking about Naomi and Joseph and Aaron and the others who will benefit from the extra sales. We made more money this year than in any previous year by a long shot."

"We don't set our store on the importance of money. The Lord provides."

Elam's hands trembled. "I understand. This isn't a matter of greed or personal gain, though. These bills will come. The doctors will charge for their services, as will the hospitals and therapists. Now we have a good deal of money in the bank. The Lord has provided. But just as we plow the fields and plant our crops, we do our share to see that we can pay those to whom we owe money."

Naomi touched his shoulder, and a zing raced down his back. "May I say something?"

The bishop nodded, his arms crossed in front of him.

Naomi spoke in a voice soft and gentle as the wind. "While I don't condone what Elam did, I understand his motives. He wanted to help my son and many others in the district.

He only had my welfare and that of so many others in mind. In the end, it turned out fine. No one nosed around here. At the end of the day, the Englisch all left. It's done and over with, without any additional interference. Elam shouldn't have told my story without my permission, but nothing bad happened because of it."

That zing that zapped through his spine now raced throughout his body. She defended him. He bit back the laughter that bubbled in his chest. Could it be that she forgave him?

"My word is to be obeyed."

At the bishop's proclamation, the chuckle stuck in Elam's throat. He sucked in a deep breath. "*Ja*, it is. And from now on, I will follow what you say."

"Can you?" The bishop scrunched his gray eyebrows together. "I've heard it so often from your mouth that I question the truth of it. You might say it now, but what happens the next time you want to go your own way?"

Could he follow the bishop's directives when he had this habit of running off and doing whatever he wanted, no matter what the man said? "All I can say is that I'll try."

The bishop harrumphed. "Trying is not enough. There must be doing on your part. I will consult with the elders on this matter.

You haven't proven yourself to be an asset to the district. We will decide what to do about your future, whether we let you stay. For the time being, keep out of trouble. This is the last I want to hear of your antics. Do I make myself clear?"

Elam nodded, and then stared at his feet.

"*Gut*. Now, I need a piece of my wife's chocolate crazy cake." He turned and left, his step as strong and determined as when he'd marched to confront Elam.

He released a breath he hadn't realized he'd been holding. His future in the district and his life with Naomi hung in the balance. The bishop and elders would determine his path for the rest of his days. A burning churning filled his gut. He turned back to Rachel and Naomi, who rocked Joseph in her arms. "What am I going to do?"

She straightened the *bobbeli's* lightweight blanket. "If you truly want to be Amish, you are going to have to start obeying the bishop and the Ordnung. For your sake, I hope you do. Now it's time for me to feed Joseph. Think about everything we've said today."

She and Rachel went into the house, the screen door clapping shut behind them. He sagged to the step and sat down, rubbing his temples. *Ja*, he'd heard what the bishop and

Naomi said. What he was most sorry about was hurting her. That, he never intended. He'd truly meant it for her good, not for her harm.

What did his future hold? A life with Naomi or a life alone?

Chapter Seventeen

With the din of the bakery swirling around her, Naomi stood over the fryer, dropping in raised doughnuts one at a time until the vat filled. The reek of hot oil and steaming dough overtook her. Not to mention the heat, even though the cement-block basement walls kept the room cooler than the upstairs. She wriggled her bare toes on the chilly cement floor. Out front, customers would be winding their way through the tiny shop, picking out loaves of bread, pies and cinnamon rolls to consume either on the picnic tables set on the grass or once they got home.

Truth be told, it was nice to be out of earshot of Joseph for a few hours. He wasn't sleeping well. Without the aid of a doctor, Mamm diagnosed his sleeping problems. Her *bobbeli* was teething. The first razor-sharp tooth erupted last week. Even knowing what caused him to cry so much didn't make for better rest. He still had her walking the floor with him at the oddest hours of the night. She shook her head to keep awake so she didn't burn the doughnuts.

She rubbed her eyes and focused her attention on the bubbling oil in front of her.

"You'd better turn those before you have an over-fried mess on your hands." Rachel's words pierced through Naomi's groggy haze.

"What? Oh, sorry." She flipped them just in time to avoid having to toss the entire batch.

"You're clearly done in. Why don't you go home?"

"I'm not sure Mamm would let me through the door." Naomi gave a wry laugh.

"Your mamm will understand. I take it Joseph is still keeping you up at night?"

"*Ja.* Then he sleeps during the day, but I can't stay in bed. Chores don't wait until *bobbelin* finish teething. Which I hope is soon. So do Aaron, Laura, Sam and everyone else in the house."

Sylvia came up behind them and squeezed Naomi's shoulder. "I overheard that." She set her jaw. "I'm going to insist that you leave. If you doze off, you might fall in the oil."

"I agree." Rachel narrowed her eyes and frowned in a failed attempt at sternness.

"I'm not quite that tired." Naomi yawned.

"There, now I've caught you in a lie." Sylvia steered her by the shoulders toward the doorway.

"But did you see the line today? It's up the hill to the parking lot. It's Friday, people are on vacation, and the weather is sunny and warm. You need an extra pair of hands."

"You can leave your hands. The rest of you needs to go home."

Naomi couldn't help but giggle. "You have the strangest sense of humor. That's why I love the two of you so."

"I'm glad I made you laugh. Now, if I can make you rest, my day will be complete. Go on. Rachel has to get back to those doughnuts, and I have pretzels to twist."

"*Denki* for being so understanding about everything. I will make it up to you, Sylvia." Naomi washed her hands and snuck out of the kitchen and into the narrow hallway used as a storeroom.

She opened the door to step out, ready to take a breath of clean summer air, but Elam blocked her way. She tingled all over at the sight of him. *Nein*, she had to stop this nonsense. He was not whom she wanted to run into today. She had to protect herself.

"Where are you off to? Isn't it your day to work?" He stood in front of her, lean and muscular and tanned. Her traitorous heart did a flip.

She shifted her feet in the dirt, avoiding eye contact with him. "*Ja*, but Joseph's teething has been keeping me up at night. Sylvia shooed me out and told me to take a nap."

"That's too bad. Not about your going home to rest, but about Joseph teething. Mamm has some dry rusks in the house for when Mary brings her little guy over. I'll get you some."

For whatever reason, she couldn't bring herself to tell him they'd bought some last week. "I thought you started with the construction company again."

"I did. It's tradition that the new guy on the job brings a treat for the crew. Even though I've worked with this company before, I am the latest hire, so I thought I'd bring them hand pies. Vern, another guy on the crew who brings me back and forth to work, drove me and said he'd be back after the lunch hour."

She hadn't told him about the Herschbergers' offer. Not after the fiasco at the auction. Not after he went behind her back and hurt her again.

A white van with the words *News Station* emblazoned across it in blue and red pulled into the driveway. Naomi went cold. "What are they doing here?"

Elam spun, and then fidgeted with his hat's brim. "Probably doing a story in the area and stopped by for a treat." He gulped. "I'm sure that's all it is."

But his falter told her otherwise. "Did you contact them, too?"

"They're a television station. I only went to the papers. Why would I want to talk to anyone on TV?"

"A television station?" Her mouth went dry.

A fair-haired woman stepped from the van, her dress clinging to her every curve, her lips painted a bright red. A darker man followed and reached back in for a large video camera with a fuzzy microphone on top. They sauntered toward the line of customers that snaked out the door and up the little hill toward the parking lot. The woman leaned toward the man and said something to him.

Naomi shivered. "I don't have a *gut* feeling about this."

Sure enough, the two reporters skirted the line and headed toward Elam and Naomi. She grabbed him by the arm and hissed at him. "You did this. Now undo it."

* * *

Elam kept his eyes on the Englisch couple who strode in their direction. The man wore jeans and a casual blue button-down shirt, but the woman wore a navy-blue jacket and skirt and teetered through the grass in high heels. They headed straight for Elam and Naomi, the only Amish people in sight.

Beside him, Naomi sucked in a breath and stiffened. He reached to grab her by the hand, but she pulled away, her fingers icy cold. That chill ran up his arm and straight to his heart.

He sighed. The news station probably got the idea for a story from one of the newspapers. The newspapers *he'd* contacted and given the interviews. So again, his actions would hurt Naomi. His mistakes had this way of never going away. Instead, they rose from the ash heap and haunted him. Well, since he'd made this mess, it was his to clean up. He straightened and met the reporters partway. As he reached them, he glanced over his shoulder. Naomi stood rooted in place.

He cleared his throat. "Good morning."

The woman smiled. She reached to shake his hand, and he reciprocated. "Good morning. I'm Leila Richardson from Channel 9 News, and my cameraman, Jason Turnbull. Through our sources, we heard about the auction held here a couple of weeks ago and how it was to benefit a little boy who needed heart surgery. A Joseph Miller. We believe his mother works at this bakery. Naomi is her name. Do either of you know her?"

"How did you know that? They published the story anonymously."

"I have my sources. Now, if you could point me to this woman."

"Naomi, what are you still doing here?" Rachel called from behind them.

Naomi gasped.

Leila glanced over her shoulder at Jason and gave a single nod before crossing to stand in front of Naomi. Elam went and stood beside her. From the corner of his eye, he glimpsed Rachel duck back into the bakery.

A wide grin crossed the reporter's scarlet lips. Jason lifted the camera to his shoulder. "Well, it's nice to finally meet the woman behind the story. How is your son doing?"

"He's fine. Why are you here?"

Leila smoothed her perfectly curled hair. "It isn't our intent to intrude on your way of life. But many people are fascinated by the Amish, and the little boy's story in the paper several weeks ago struck a chord with them. A follow-up would be great. Just to let them know how he's getting on. I'm glad to hear he's well. Has he had his surgery?"

"I'm not sure I want to answer any of your questions."

Even though they didn't touch, Naomi stood beside Elam and trembled. He cleared his throat. "It's not our way to be interviewed on camera."

The man nodded. "We understand that. There are several options for conducting the interview. We could show you in shadow, so the audience wouldn't be able to see your faces. We could also just get the audio from you, and add in scenes from the area for the video. If that still makes you too uncomfortable, we could take a statement. Leila would do the voice-over, and again, we'd use shots of things like barns, cows and buggies."

"My son is very ill. He needs peace and quiet to get better, so that, God willing, he will grow into a strong man. Please, go away and leave us alone. That's all I have to say about any of this." With each word, her voice strained.

Elam took half a step in Leila's direction. "Respect Naomi's request. She didn't want any of this attention. I'm the one who went to the papers with the story. She had nothing to do with it. She lives a simple and quiet life and would like it kept that way. When I spoke to the reporters before the auction, I did so against her wishes. I'm sorry you came all this way for nothing, but there will be no statements, no interviews, nothing."

Leila stepped forward and touched his arm. He backed away.

"All I'm asking for is a brief statement as to the child's health. How is he doing? Is he getting better and stronger?"

He gazed at Naomi, who chewed on her lip. "That sounds like more than a brief statement. No one needs to know about my child. I don't even understand why they're so interested."

"Because everyone loves babies. They make the best human-interest stories. Since the public knows the beginning, they're clamoring for the end. I can't tell you how many requests I get each day for more information about the little boy. People stop me on the street and ask, not even realizing I didn't write the newspaper articles. That's why I'm here. Your interview will put the story to rest." Leila drew her lips into a pout. "It's only a small thing I'm asking."

"Not to me." Again, Naomi's voice cracked. She tightened her shoulders. "Are you a mother?"

Leila gave a laugh that was more like a

burst of air from her lips. "I'm a career woman, Mrs. Miller. That's my focus in life."

"Then you don't understand my need to protect my child. Do you let the world know your business?"

"It wouldn't interest them. Not like your story."

Elam fisted his hands. There had to be something he could do to stop these people and make them leave her alone. "What, other than a story, will make you go away?"

"Just share with a small corner of the world how the child is." She leaned toward him again, her words softening to an almost-purr. "And I usually get what I want, Mr...?"

Naomi gripped his forearm with a vise-like hold. "Don't you dare even think about telling them anything."

"Now, now, my dear, there's no need for such dramatics. I understand your concern for your son. But give the people what they want, and then they'll stay away. Once their appetite is satiated, they'll be content to let you go back to your regular life. If you don't speak to someone, they'll never leave you alone."

Heat rose in Elam's chest. He fought to keep his hands at his side so he wouldn't strangle the woman. "I was wrong to ever compromise Naomi's privacy. We're done speaking to the press. And you can tell everyone who works at the other television stations and newspapers the same thing. If you would please accept my apologies, I need to get back to work." Not waiting for a reply, he grabbed Naomi by the wrist and pulled her behind him toward the door.

A strident woman's voice followed them. "Did you get all of that, Jason?"

As Elam went to turn the doorknob, he froze.

"We'll be able to piece together a statement from the mother. Good work, as usual." The cameraman's voice held a hint of laughter.

"I do always get what I want. Now, let's see if we can get anyone else here to talk."

Elam spun around as they strode toward their van. He let go of Naomi and raced after them.

They hopped inside the vehicle as he got to them. "Stop. You can't put that on TV. You need a release."

Leila rolled down her window and tipped her head to the side. "Actually, we don't. You were in public."

"Please."

"Let's get out of here, Jason."

With tires spitting gravel that stung Elam's bare forearms, the news van sped from the driveway.

He stood statue-still until it disappeared down the street.

Naomi reached him, tears streaking down her face. "They can't do that, can they?"

"Maybe they can. I don't know, but I doubt there's anything we can do to stop them." He pulled her to himself and held her close.

For a brief moment, she relaxed against him. Then she tried to pull away, but he clung to her. She pounded on his chest. "Let me go. You did this. It's your fault. How could you? How could you?"

He released her.

She stumbled backward against a tree and spat her words at him. "Go away and leave me alone. I don't ever want to see you again." With that, she fled into the bakery.

The weight of the Englischers' stares pressed on Elam's shoulders.

There was only one thing he could do. Without her, staying here was pointless. Not when no one else wanted him.

He needed to leave.

Chapter Eighteen

Naomi hid just inside the bakery's back door, taking only shallow breaths until all fell quiet outside except for the low din of Englisch voices as they waited in line.

Just like the accident, Elam's going to the papers bore consequences that continued to multiply. The news story wasn't going to go away. Tonight, her face and voice would be on televisions all over Wisconsin. When would this nightmare end? Maybe reporters from Chicago or New York would hear about the story and would want to speak to her.

She concentrated on inhaling and exhaling but couldn't get a regular pattern of breathing going.

"Naomi, there you are. What are you still doing here? Elam's out front asking for you."

Sylvia wiped her hands on her apron. "*Ach*, what has happened?"

"I can't… I can't… I can't speak to him. Or to anyone." Naomi opened the door and stumbled out.

"Let me walk you home."

"I can—"

"You can't." Sylvia got that no-nonsense mother tone going. "Whatever happened has upset you something awful. You can't even stand upright. I'll help you to your place. It wouldn't do to have you hit by a car."

Out of energy to argue, Naomi leaned against Sylvia as they headed for home.

Home. The only safe place in the world. How long would it be that way? When would the outsiders come and take even that from her? She had lost so much. Her active, athletic brother. The healthy son she'd always longed for. Her husband. They had shared a deep friendship, and she missed that. The nights in the living room as he had read *The Budget* and she'd darned his socks. The easy conversation after dinner. The mornings when he'd come in from the barn and kiss her cheek as she'd handed him a cup of coffee.

Would life ever be like that again?

Elam had hurt her too many times. Over and over, he bumbled his way through life.

Always sorry for what he did. But his actions left a trail of heartache.

"This has something to do with Elam, doesn't it?" Sylvia looked both ways and led Naomi across the road.

She swiped at the tears that dribbled down her cheeks. "Doesn't it always?"

"Rachel told me about the truck."

"They're going to put us on television. I didn't know they were filming when they asked about Joseph. Even though I didn't say much, I guess it was enough for them to get their story. And again, it's Elam's fault."

"I'm sorry that had to happen, my dear. But you can't blame Elam for every one of your troubles."

Naomi stopped cold at the end of the driveway. "Why not, when he's to blame?"

"He's worked so hard to gain back your trust. I've watched him these past few months. And you. You're in love with him but afraid to take another risk in letting him into your heart."

"He's already there. And that's the problem. Each time something happens, he's always sorry. Sincerely regretful for what he did. But his choices don't affect just him. He forgets about the troubles he leaves behind for others."

"That young man loves you and would do anything for you and your son. True, he often goes about it the wrong way, but he always, always has your best interest in mind. He wants to help you, to be there for you. Can't you let him? Wouldn't it be easier to bear this burden together with him rather than to walk such a difficult road alone?"

They continued their stroll to the kitchen door. "I might as well be ripped in two. *Ja*, I love him. I do. Maybe more than ever. But I'm also scared of him. Of what disaster he's going to bring this time."

"Think about why you love him. Isn't it because of everything he's done for you and Joseph? For his thoughtfulness and his protection of you. Forget about the past, forgive him of his clumsy attempts at helping you, and forge ahead with the man I suspect you've always loved. We are not promised skies always blue but a Helper to see us through."

"*Ja*, my mamm has quoted that proverb to me many times in the past few years."

"And don't forget about what Elam must be suffering. His guilt over hurting you and Aaron presses on him. I see it in his eyes, how he softens around you, but how he also sorrows over his sins."

Naomi bit her lip. Had he suffered? How

much guilt did he carry? And he walked away from her and their district. How much that must have hurt.

"*Denki*, Sylvia. I can't have a future with Elam, but you've given me something to think about. I'm done in. If I don't get a nap, Rachel is going to scold me like a hen clucks after her chicks."

Like a grossmammi, Sylvia patted Naomi's cheek. "Rest well. Things always look different after some sleep."

Naomi entered the house and clicked the door shut behind her.

No one bustled about the kitchen. The stove sat cold. Maybe Mamm would make a tuna salad or something along those lines tonight. With the heat, it would be too much to cook. The table, the floors, the counters, everything in the room was clean and tidy. Just as it should be. The way it always should be. Welcoming. Home. "Hello? Is anyone here?"

Only the steady ticking of the clock in the living room broke the silence. Where was everyone? And Joseph? She moved to climb the stairs when Aaron rolled in from the back hall.

"I thought you were working today."

"Rachel and Sylvia sent me home to take a nap. Since Joseph hasn't been sleeping well, they were afraid I would doze off and wind up in the fryer."

He smiled, the dimple she'd been envious of as a child deepening in his cheek. "In that case, it is best you came home."

"Where is everyone?"

"Mamm and Laura took Joseph and went to visit Nancy Yoder. You heard she had a baby girl last night?"

"It was all the talk at the bakery." The Amish grapevine spread that word around before the *bobbeli* was fifteen minutes old. "Did you come in for a reason?"

"Daed wanted some lemonade, if there's any made up. It's awfully hot in the shed today, even with the doors open."

"I think there is. Will you just take the jug?"

"*Ja.* And maybe whatever blueberry pie is left from last night."

"I'll get it for you." Good to take her mind off what had just happened.

"Did I see a news van parked outside the bakery?"

"*Ja.*"

"Did they stop for some doughnuts or Danish?"

"*Nein.* And I'm not sure I want to get into it."

"Did those reporters want to talk to you?"

"It's a long story that I'll share tonight so I only have to tell it one time. But in a word, *ja*."

Aaron rolled to the table, took off his hat and set it down. "You're tired, and you need a nap, but I'm glad we're alone. If you have a minute, I'd like to speak to you."

"Sounds serious. What about?"

"Elam."

With her knees refusing to support her, she leaned against the Formica counter, chipped in a few places by years of hard use. "I don't want to talk about him."

"What I don't understand is why no one in the district or in this house, even, is willing to let go of the past and accept him."

"How can you ask that? Look at you. You'll never be able to walk again, never be able to handle a plow, never stroll with a girl by the river. Every day, you're a reminder of what happened. Of Elam's poor choices. So is that news truck that showed up today."

"We all make bad decisions in our lives. Haven't you eaten something that made you sick, goofed off instead of getting your work done, got upset with someone you love?"

"Don't we all? But those consequences aren't as severe or as permanent and don't affect people the way his choices do."

"Forgiveness is a *wunderbaar* thing, Naomi. And forgetting. That doesn't mean some reminders don't remain, but it does mean choosing to look beyond the past to the present and future. I found a Bible verse the other day that astonished me, that gave me some perspective on the entire matter. I've been bitter about the accident, but this helped me see the situation in a different light."

She stared at her brother, sitting broken in his chair. His face had lost its boyishness, replaced by a certain strength that matured him. He wasn't a child anymore, but a man. One God had given a great deal of wisdom. "What is it?"

"Isaiah 43:25. *'I, even I, am he that blotteth out thy transgressions for mine own sake, and will not remember thy sins.'* If God can forget, why can't we?"

The question hit Naomi in the gut.

Elam slammed the suitcase onto his bed, where it bounced for a moment before coming to rest. He flung open the wardrobe door, his handmade shirts hanging pressed and neat. What was the point in packing? Where he was going, he wouldn't need his Amish clothes.

And this time, he wouldn't be back.

He'd tried this before, leaving the past here to forget. No matter how hard he worked at it, he never got Naomi out of his mind or heart. He thought about her all day long, dreamed about her every night.

But staying in the district would be pure torture. To hear her voice but not be able to speak to her. To smell her sweet fragrance, but not be able to hold her close. She didn't want him here. That much, she'd made clear. She had turned her back on him once more. And the bishop was likely to tell him to leave.

He sighed. From the bottom of the last drawer, he drew out his blue jeans and a plain green button-down shirt. Beside those items sat his tennis shoes. They stared at him, almost daring him to lace them on and to walk away for good.

He squeezed his eyes shut. Did he have the courage to step through that door, never to return to live this lifestyle, even if it was one he believed in? Or did he have the greater courage to stay here and fight for his dreams and for the woman he loved?

Right now, he didn't have the gumption for either. He slumped to the floor, dropping the clothing next to himself. *Oh, God, I don't know what to do.*

Perhaps his sins were too great even for the Lord to forgive.

He heaved himself from the floor and placed his Englisch clothes in the suitcase, and then closed it with a click. If he left here in his Amish pants and shirt, maybe Mamm wouldn't be so brokenhearted.

He didn't want to know what Daed would think.

The house was quiet and empty. Daed must be at work on those account books again. This was the better way. Right now, he had to get to work. From Chase's house tonight, he'd phone Frank and have him deliver the message to Mamm and Daed.

Once in the barn, he moved to the back of the building where his truck sat, covered with a tarp to protect it from dust. He grazed over the passenger-side headlight, the area where he'd struck the tree. The accident had happened so fast.

Aaron had sat behind him, his window opened to the late-fall warmth. "You know what I could go for?"

Elam held on to the steering wheel as they bumped over the road. "Hmm?"

"A pizza. Don't you have your phone? You could call ahead to that one place that has the deep-dish kind, and we can pick it up to go.

My mouth is watering." Typical for a sixteen-year-old guy.

"Sounds *gut* to me. What do you want on it?"

"Everything. Pepperoni, sausage, mushrooms, onions, green peppers. Just tell them to leave off the olives."

Elam reached into the cup holder for his cell. He fiddled to unlock it, and then with one hand typed the name of the restaurant into the search engine.

"Elam! Watch out!"

When he peered up, the tree was right there.

More screams.

The crunch of metal.

And nothing but silence.

The nickering of the buggy horse brought him back to the present. That night would haunt him forever.

He shook his head to clear the images and threw his battered suitcase into the backseat.

Daed shuffled in from the office. "Where are you going?"

"To work."

"Vern picks you up."

"He'll be here soon. I'll follow him."

"Why would you do that?"

A slicing pain cut through Elam's head. He

leaned against the truck. "Let's face it, Daed. No one in the district is going to accept me. Not the bishop, not Naomi. Not even you. It's time for me to leave."

"For good?"

All Elam could manage was a nod.

"You're running away from your problems again."

Elam held his breath for a moment, then released it a little at a time. Was that what he was doing?

"It's what you always do. When you face a hard time in your life, you take off. But trouble will hunt you down and never let you go."

"What else am I supposed to do when the people here all but shun me?"

"Do you want to be here?"

"*Ja*, of course I do. I never meant to turn my back on this district in the first place. But no one can forget. And all I do is make mistake after mistake." His throat tightened, but he forced the words through the narrow passage. "It's best that I leave, so I don't ruin any more lives."

Daed held on to the truck bed with his left hand. "You haven't seen it yet, have you? You don't understand."

"What?" Elam walked in a circle, removed

his hat and finger-combed his hair. "What is it that I don't get?"

"Why you aren't accepted. Why you haven't integrated into the district no matter how hard you try."

"And you aren't going to tell me, are you?" He blew out a breath. "You're going to make me figure it out on my own, like you always have."

"Do you even want to know?"

"Of course I do."

Daed nodded. "Without raising your voice, tell me what you desire."

Elam forced himself to relax his shoulders. "I want to be a member of this district. I want to open my own outdoor furniture shop, and I want to marry Naomi Miller." The strength of that desire astonished him. He did love her. Always had. Always would. "Because without any of that, I have nothing." His stomach burned.

His gray-haired father stroked his beard with his good hand. "Then I will tell you. Come into the office."

Elam followed Daed to the back of the barn and positioned himself on the squeaky office chair.

"You've been home, what, four or five months now? You say you want to rejoin the district, but you haven't been baptized yet. Do you intend to go through with it?"

"I did. But with planning the auction and taking care of the farm, and after the fiasco with the newspapers, I didn't get around to it."

"A solemn commitment like that shouldn't be something you do when you get around to it. That should be your first priority. If you're serious, do it. Not for Naomi's sake or for the chance to be accepted here, but because you want to live and practice the Amish way of life and our beliefs." Daed sipped from a glass of water on the corner of the neat desk. "Think about that for a while. If you value this way of life, if it's what you truly want, don't leave. Stay here, make that commitment and fight for what you want."

Did he have the fight left in him?

Elam drew in a deep breath. Running away hadn't worked before. Should he stay? Could he?

"Prove yourself to be a man who faces the consequences of his actions. That's what being grown-up and mature is all about. It's what a woman wants in a husband."

Daed was right. Hadn't Naomi even told him he needed to think more? "I'll stay at least for a couple of days while I think about this. Vern will be here soon to take me back to work."

He left the barn, but Daed's words rang in his head. Was part of the reason the community—and Naomi—didn't accept him because he hadn't made a commitment to the district?

Was he ready to take that step? He loved the Lord. He believed in this way of life. The yearning he had as a younger man for the things of the outside world had faded.

Frank had a bumper stick on his van, a verse that had always made Elam stop and think. What did it say again? *"Believe on the Lord Jesus Christ, and thou shalt be saved."*

Believe. That was about it.

He brought his suitcase inside, put it away and went downstairs. While he waited for Vern, he grabbed the big, well-worn family Bible from the small table beside Daed's chair. He flipped through the book of Acts, searching for the passage. Scanning each page, he flipped them over until he came to the fifteenth chapter, in which Peter spoke to the apostles and elders. He said, *"But we believe that through the grace of the Lord Jesus Christ we shall be saved, even as they."*

There it was again. So plain. So simple. All his striving, was it for nothing? Could he ever do enough to earn his forgiveness? This verse and the one on Frank's van both spoke simply of believing.

Nothing else.

A lightness filled him, one that had never occupied his soul, even before the accident. The truth of it weakened his knees and sent his heart scampering.

To be accepted and forgiven by God, he had to do nothing other than believe.

Headlights swept through the living room, shining on the wall behind Elam. When had it gotten so dark? He peered out the window. Large, heavy, rain-laden clouds filled the sky. Vern, strong and active despite the creeping up of years, sprinted for the house. Elam let him in before he even knocked.

He fussed with his Milwaukee Brewers baseball cap. "They told me at the bakery they'd seen you headed here. The boss has stopped work for the day. Some pretty nasty storms are expected, so we'll get a few hours off. I'll see you in the morning."

"Thank you for coming to let me know. See you tomorrow."

Vern left, and Elam thumped down into Daed's lumpy chair. Free time. Then he could go do what he should have done months ago.

Chapter Nineteen

Lightning sizzled across the sky, followed on its heels by peals of thunder rolling one after the other. Rain lashed the windows, and wind bent the trees like little old ladies.

By the light of the gas lamp, Elam read Daed's Bible, consuming the words of hope. Of forgiveness. Of reconciliation. All of that was possible with God. He closed the book and eased back in the chair, letting it all sink it. Allowing it to take root in his heart and grow.

In the midst of the storm without and the calm within, a knock came at the door. What was that? Elam rose from his chair. The knocking sounded once more, and then again as he made his way through the kitchen.

There, at the door at the top of the ramp,

was Aaron. "About time you answered. Can I come in?"

Elam moved to the side and allowed Aaron to enter. "Come in."

"*Denki*. This is a nasty storm."

Elam threw Aaron a dish towel to dry off and hustled outside, pulling Aaron's buggy and horse into the barn. He returned to the house, bucking the wind the entire way. "You must be crazy to be out in this weather."

Aaron handed the towel back to Elam. "Daed needed to me to pick up a batch of drawer pulls he ordered from Paul at the smithy. Took longer than I thought it would, but I figured I could beat the storm home. Guess I was wrong. Thanks for taking me in."

"No one should be out right now. You had *gut* sense to stop."

"I'm glad the storm hit when it did. I've wanted to talk to you for a while now, but it never seemed like the right time or place. I take it your mamm went to see the new baby?"

"Isn't that where all the women are?" Elam chuckled. "Nancy doesn't have to worry about the *bobbeli* keeping her from getting any rest. The visitors will see to that, say not?"

Aaron joined the laughter. "For sure and

certain. The prescription for childbirth is a casserole. The cheesier, the better."

"But that's not what you want to speak to me about, I'm guessing."

"Nein." Aaron's laughter faded away, taking his smile with it.

Elam swallowed hard. Maybe he'd heard about the run-in with the news crew. Even with the district's women occupied, word must have spread. No doubt Naomi told him before he left for the smithy.

"I've been doing some thinking about my future. What I want the rest of my life to look like. And it comes down to this. I don't want to work for my daed anymore. You've encourage me and shown me what I can do. I want more for myself."

"Why not?" Elam furrowed his forehead. "You have everything you need there, all the equipment, and your daed is a *gut* teacher. If he could show me how to be a carpenter, he can show you."

Aaron leaned forward on the couch. "That's the problem. You have some kind of idea of how stubborn he is."

Elam nodded. Did he ever.

"He won't listen to me. He's afraid the work will be too much for me, that I'll get sick or hurt. We've had numerous discussions about this. Nothing has changed."

"I know what it's like to run into brick walls with people, to have them not give you a fair chance. But what does this have to do with me?"

"Naomi tells me you want to start your own outdoor furniture shop. Make things like chairs and tables and the like."

"Ja." Elam strung out the word to give himself time to formulate what he had to say next. "But I don't have a shop. No equipment other than a few hand tools and a diesel engine. My daed is just about as stubborn as yours. He still hasn't given me an answer to my idea to use a corner of the barn to get started. That's why I'm back on the construction crew. I'd love to give you a job, but right now, I don't have a business."

Aaron shivered.

Elam jumped up. "I'm not a very *gut* host. Let me pour you some coffee. Mamm always keeps the pot warm on the back of the stove." He went to the kitchen, poured a cup for Aaron and one for himself, and returned to the living room. "Do you need dry clothes, too? I'm sorry to keep you sitting in wet things."

"That might be *gut.*"

Elam got some of his own clothes and Aaron rolled to the bedroom to change. While he did, Elam paced the living room. Aaron was taking his time getting to the point. What did he want from him? Surely he didn't want to leave the Amish, did he? Might he think that Elam would take him with him and help him find work, maybe with Chase? If that was the case, what would Elam say to him?

After a few minutes, Aaron returned to the living room.

"That must feel better."

"For sure."

"I'm still trying to guess what this all has to do with me."

"I have some money saved from working for Daed, and I'd like to invest it. In you."

Elam stumbled backward and sat in Mamm's rocker with a thump. "In me?"

"I'd like to be partners with you. We might be able to find a little space and get a few tools to get us going. If you'll have me, that is."

The world spun around Elam. He couldn't have heard right. "Why would you want to go into business with me after what I did to you?"

"Because I've forgiven you."

"But you can't forget." Elam's windpipe tightened. "You'll never be able to forget."

"I can."

Elam stared at the sandy-haired man. In the three years he'd been gone, Aaron had grown into a fine young person. Wise beyond his age. Perhaps in times to come, when Bishop Zook was gone, the lot might fall to Aaron to fill that role. Elam could see it. "You have a heart I will never understand."

"I've had plenty of time to read the Bible and think and pray. God has helped me to see many things."

"Like what?"

"That forgiveness is freeing. Putting the past into the past and keeping it there erases all the bitterness and leaves nothing but peace and joy. If God forgives and forgets, why can't we?"

Warmth ran from Elam's head to his toes. He grinned like a young boy with a fistful of candy. "I would love to have you come into partnership with me, but I can't accept your money. You need it more than I do. Later in the fall, I should have enough saved to get my own shop and equipment. But *denki* for the offer, from the bottom of my heart. And when I'm up and running, I'll hire you first thing. I can't say anything more. Your generosity is overwhelming."

"I'm not giving you the money, I'm investing it. I'd like to be equal partners with you."

Elam hugged himself. This couldn't be true. "If that's the case, I'd love to go into business with you. *Denki*."

Aaron's grin matched Elam's. "*Nein, denki* for doing this with me. I'm excited to get going, to be out on my own and have some independence. It's a *gut* feeling."

"What is your daed going to say?"

"That's a great question. He might be upset for a while, but he'll see in the end that it's best for me."

A little bit of the lightness left Elam. This decision had further implications, including another reason for Leroy Bontrager to dislike him.

The early evening summer air was soft, the moon large in the eastern sky, the sun touching the western horizon as Naomi drove her buggy along the quiet road. Joseph slept beside her. This moment of peace and quiet was rare. She breathed in the scent of hay and someone's barbecue. Her mouth watered.

A few more days, and she would move into the *dawdi haus*. Finally be on her own with her son. And with his surgery coming soon, she could get back to living a somewhat normal life.

She spurred the horse on. Time to get home and get Joseph settled in his crib. She glanced at him, his little mouth puckering as he dreamed. He'd want to be fed soon.

The clip-clop of the horse lulled her. And then came a thump. Her buggy tilted to one side. Oh great. The wheel must have broken. Now what was she going to do?

Leaving Joseph still sleeping, she slipped from the buggy and surveyed the damage. Sure enough, one of the spokes had snapped. She peered up and down the road. Nothing but emptiness. Not many drove this quiet stretch of street. She paced along the graveled shoulder. How was she going to get home? How long before someone came by?

Joseph woke up and wailed. She unbuckled him from the car seat and jiggled him. Tears still rolled down his thin cheeks. His cry ramped up.

No matter how much she talked to him or walked with him, he wouldn't calm down. His cries filled her ears and tore at her soul. It must be the teething. And not a car in sight. No houses along this stretch of marshy road.

But with Joseph continuing to wail, she might have to hike to find a phone. She shivered.

Tears welled in her own eyes. She pinched her nose to keep them at bay, but a few managed to trickle down her face. She swiped them away. Crying wouldn't help the situation. Forcing herself to take a deep breath, she concentrated on formulating a plan. And couldn't come up with anything other than walking to the nearest home and praying the people would be kind.

Then the clip-clop of hooves on asphalt cut through Joseph's sobbing. She blinked away the moisture and cleared her vision. An Amish buggy. Who?

As it approached, the driver waved at her. Elam. How was it that he showed up just when she needed him? Or when she didn't want him. All the time, really. Strong. Reliable.

Her heart hurt. She was tired of the ups and downs of life, of trying to walk through each day alone. She was tired of pushing him away. Of being angry with him. Truth be told, she missed him.

He pulled beside her and reined the horse to a stop. "Need some help?"

Now the tears came fast and furious. Along with her son, she sobbed.

"*Ach*, Naomi." He jumped down and wrapped her and Joseph in an embrace.

She leaned into him, his strong arms around her, protecting her. Right now, she was too tired to fight it. To fight him anymore. Sylvia had said she should allow Elam to help her carry this burden. And in this moment, she would let him.

"What's wrong?"

"Everything. I'm tired of hurting, of blaming, of dredging up the past."

"Put the past in the past and keep it there," he whispered into her hair.

His soft words calmed Joseph. And her. She peered at him through tear-laced lashes. "Is it that easy?"

"Can things ever be the way they once were?"

At the pain in her chest, she sucked in her breath. "*Nein*, Elam, we can't go back to the past, no matter how much we may want it. We can't deny all that has happened."

"And neither can we move forward, can we?" With a grunt, he stepped away from her. "Why, Naomi, why? You turned your back on me after the accident, never giving me a chance to explain. Never giving me a chance to apologize. If only you had listened to me."

A groan escaped her lips. "I couldn't. Not

then. Not when Aaron was suffering. And you didn't stay around long enough for me to get to the place where I could hear what you had to say."

"And now?"

Once more, she rested against him. "I think it's time to do that. To let go of it all."

His breath brushed her cheek. "Can you?"

"If I truly want to live and to love again, I have to." Her pulse pounded in her ears.

"Then I'm only going to ask you this one more time. Naomi Miller, do you forgive me for injuring your brother, for running away and leaving you, for sharing your private story with the world?"

The corners of her lips turned up. "*Ja*, Elam, I forgive you."

A truck whizzed by, one similar to Elam's, the breeze of it whipping her skirt around her knees. What was she doing, standing in the middle of the road hugging Elam Yoder? She pulled herself from his embrace. Joseph whimpered. "I put the past in the past, like you said. But there can be no future for us. I'm sorry if I gave you the wrong impression just now. Could you fix the buggy? Or take me somewhere I can call for help?"

He bowed his head a fraction of an inch

and stared at the blacktop, his shoulders slumped. "Why not?"

"Please, I don't want to talk about it." Joseph revved up for another good cry. "Just get me home."

The forgiving part was *gut*. A lightness filled her chest that hadn't been there for years.

But the ache that gripped her heart didn't ease.

Chapter Twenty

With shaking, sweaty hands, Elam knocked on Bishop Zook's door. This was the last move for him to make. For himself. For the district. For Naomi.

Martha Zook opened the door, her black apron covering her round middle. Crinkles formed at the corner of her eyes as she smiled. "How good to see you, Elam."

This was the warmest reception he'd had from just about anyone in the area since his return other than the Herschbergers. Did she have some inkling as to why he was here?

"I just finished the frosting on a chocolate crazy cake. Come in and have a slice. And I'll pour you a nice cold glass of milk."

Elam's mouth watered at the thought. Martha Zook was known throughout the area and beyond for her chocolate crazy cake. She had a secret ingredient that made it the most sought-after dessert at any church function.

"While your offer is the most tempting one I've received recently, this isn't a social call. I need to speak to your husband. Is he around?"

"If the buggy's in the yard, I expect you'll find him in the greenhouse. He's probably out there watering all his little mum plants."

"*Denki.* It was good to see you."

"The offer of cake still stands. When you finish with Reuben, come back and have a piece. Don't leave it for just the two of us. Goodness knows I don't need it all."

The Lord had never granted Reuben and Martha Zook any children, but they treated the *kinner* of the district, each and every one of them, as their own. And, in Martha's case, that included Elam. He wandered across the yard, behind the barn and around the field of feed corn to the large, rectangular greenhouse at the edge of the Zook property. The bishop sold perennials, annuals and vegetables in the spring, but he was best known for the beauty and variety of the mums he brought out in the fall. Elam stepped into the warm, sun-filled building.

Sure enough, there was Bishop Zook pushing a dolly with a hug blue plastic water tank on it, dipping into it every so often and watering his plants.

"Bishop Zook."

The older man waved at Elam. "I'll be right there. Let me finish this row so I don't lose my place."

The delay did nothing for Elam's nerves. A colony of butterflies—*nein*, maybe bumblebees—danced in his stomach. His hands shook more than when he'd knocked at their door. And the sweat dripping down his face was not from the heat in the building. What if the bishop said no? "Take your time." But hurry up.

While the bishop tended to his plants, Elam paced, his hands stuffed in his pockets, until he had a neat trench worn into the soft sand.

Bishop Zook made his way down the aisle between the flats of greens, stopping to pick a dead leaf or two. "Well, Elam, to what do I owe this visit?"

"Can we go somewhere to sit and talk?" His legs wouldn't hold him upright much longer.

"Sure. Before I left the house, Martha told me she was making a crazy cake. It must be about done. We can have a piece and chat."

"I'd rather it be in private."

"Ah." The bishop strung out the word like it

had five or six syllables. "Let's go to the barn. We can pull up a couple of bales of straw."

Elam followed the older man to the barn and situated himself on a bale across from him. The straw prickled his backside through his heavy cotton pants, and he squirmed, unable to get comfortable.

"Now, tell me the reason why you've come."

When he attempted to form the words, Elam's voice cracked. He cleared his throat and tried again. "I've come to do something that I should have done months ago. Years ago, really. And I think it will affect what you and the elders decide about me."

Bishop Zook nodded, his thin lips straight, his clear blue eyes narrow. "What is it?"

If he didn't blurt out the words right now, he'd never say them. "I've come to confess that I've been wrong about many things in my life." Elam's heart hammered against his ribs faster than any man could swing a mallet.

"Go on."

"When I was a young, I was headstrong and foolish. When people call me *grossfeelich*, they're right. I am too big for my britches. I was wrong to own a truck and a cell phone. And on that one night, I was wrong to be driving and ordering pizza on that phone. Aaron Bontrager's paralysis is my fault, and for that, I am sorry. I confess my sin before you and before God."

Did one corner of the bishop's mouth rise the tiniest of amounts?

Elam drew in another breath. "And I was wrong to go to the press with Naomi's story after both you and she had forbidden it. Like Abraham with Hagar, I rushed ahead of the Lord, wanting to give Him a helping hand instead of waiting for Him to bless the auction. Of that sin, I also repent before you and before God."

All the air rushed out of Elam's lungs, and he hunched his shoulders, never taking his sight from the bishop's face. Would he forgive him?

Yet a heavy board lifted from his shoulders, from his chest. A rush of air filled him. Did it matter if any man forgave him when the Lord already had?

The bishop stroked his beard and gazed at Elam long and hard. "Are you sincere in your repentance?"

"Ja." Hadn't he sounded like he was genuine? "Every word I said, I meant. All this time, I've been an impetuous and reckless young man. I understand now that forgiveness must first come from the Lord. That His

cleansing is the most *wunderbaar* gift of all."
He blew out a breath.

"I see." Bishop Zook's gaze didn't waver
for a moment. "What you've done is very serious, Elam. You weren't a member of the
church when you had your truck, but you
caused a disastrous accident that had serious consequences."

"I'm aware of that. Yet Aaron doesn't hold
any bitterness toward me. He has forgiven
me. And forgotten my sins against him."

"The more present problem is your unwill-
ingness to submit to my authority. Do you
want to be baptized and join the church?"

"*Ja.* That is why I've come to confess to
you today."

"As a member of the Amish church, you
would be under obligation to obey my instructions, no matter how unfair or unjust you
think they are. If you have any reservations
about that, then I suggest you not join. To be
placed under the *bann* is a most difficult thing
for a family. And a church."

"I understand."

"You aren't doing this just to get into
Naomi Miller's good graces, are you?"

"*Nein*, not at all. I'm doing this for myself alone." But how would Naomi react to
his baptism?

Bishop Zook nodded. "This is a matter that I must think on and pray about. One that I don't take lightly, and you shouldn't either."

"I never would."

"Give me time. I'll let you know later what my decision is." Bishop Zook stood up and brushed the straw from the back of his pants. "Now, let's go get a slice of Martha's crazy cake. She makes the best I've ever tasted, say not?"

How would Elam swallow while his future remained unclear? If only the bishop would hurry up and make his decision.

The warmth and conversation of the bakery swirled around Naomi as she kneaded the dough that would become a loaf of seven-grain bread, turning it over and over. Like she rolled the idea of loving Elam around in her mind.

Because she did. More now than ever. When they were engaged before, they'd both been young and maybe not truly ready for marriage, at least not to each other. She turned to Rachel, who kneaded dough for cinnamon raisin bread. "Do you ever wonder about if life happened differently?"

"What do you mean?"

"Like, what if the accident never happened and I had married Elam?"

Rachel blew a loose strand of hair from her face. "You wouldn't have Joseph."

Naomi sucked in a breath. "You're right. I never thought about that."

"God has His reasons and His ways. They aren't ours to know."

What would her life be like without Joseph? Not to see his sweet smile in the morning? Not to hear his laughter when his grossdaadi made faces at him? Not to smell his sweet powder smell when she held him close? "That's true. God has His reasons and His ways. And maybe He means for me to have a new life now with Elam."

Rachel stopped her work and turned to Naomi. "I've watched you the past week or so, and you seem happier. More at peace. Is that because you've made a decision about him?"

"I don't know. Trusting him is hard. Surrendering completely, you know. If I commit to him, I want it to be with my whole heart and for the right reasons. And I don't want to doubt him, not ever again. That isn't the way to build a marriage. If I can't do that, I have no right to be joined to him."

"What are you going to do?"

"I told him the other night that there couldn't be a future for us. But I said it because I was scared."

"Is it time for you to let go of that fear, leave what happened behind, and step out in faith?" Rachel's words were soft but demanded an answer.

As if he'd heard them talking about him, Elam strolled into the bakery. All of the women turned toward him. Many of them still held a hardness toward him. But what had started as an impenetrable wall between her and Elam melted like the ice on a warm spring day. When she saw him now, her heart didn't ache, but it fluttered in her chest.

"*Gut morgan*, everyone." He wound his way to the side of the large table where Naomi stood. "Is there a pie I can buy to take to work with me? I want to treat the crew on the job site."

"You're very early this morning. We aren't even open yet."

"I have to get to work."

"Take your pick, then." She nodded in the direction of the wire racks in the front room where the customers lined up for their goods.

He made his selection, a crust loaded with blueberries and topped with crumble, and came back to her. "Will you walk me out? I have something I want to discuss with you."

"Just give me a minute." She set the dough in a greased bowl, covered it and set it in a warm place to rise. Struggling to keep up with his long strides, she followed him outside.

The wind rattled the branches in the trees. Elam studied the sky for a moment before turning his attention to her. He gazed at her, intense, and breathed through his mouth.

What was it? Was he leaving again? Her pulse raced.

"I went to the bishop about a week ago."

"Oh." She couldn't draw in so much as a puff of air.

"We had a long talk. About the past and the future."

Wouldn't he just come out and say what he needed to tell her? That the other night was their last goodbye. That he was walking away from her once more.

He rubbed his cheek. "I went to him asking for forgiveness for everything I've done. The accident. Leaving. Going to the papers. All of it. It felt so *wunderbaar*. Even though I know God has forgiven me, I still want the people around me to do the same. And I want to be baptized."

The world tilted. Did Elam see the pulse pounding in her neck? "And what did the bishop have to say?"

"He hasn't given me an answer yet. Who knows what that means? I can only pray that he will accept my confession."

"That would be *gut* for you if he did." Her tongue stuck to the roof of her mouth.

"And maybe for you. Is there any hope at all for us? You said the other night there wasn't, but I have to ask one more time. You've forgiven me, and I'm so grateful for that. Could you consider…maybe…loving me again?"

She trembled. Could she? Really, she didn't have to ask herself the question. She knew her answer, even though she'd denied it to herself. Rachel was right. The time had come to take a step forward.

"I've done a lot of thinking since that night by the side of the road. I discovered that I do still love you, Elam Yoder. That hasn't changed. This time, though, my love is more cautious, more mature."

He nodded and caressed her cheek, a shiver shooting through her. "You know I never stopped loving you. Each and every day, I thought of you. You're what drew me back."

"I'm glad you came. But I hope you aren't doing this for me." She touched his forearm, tingles racing up her own. "You need to do this for yourself. To find your own peace and your own place here."

"That is why I went to the bishop."

"And what happens if he refuses to baptize you?"

"Do you think he will?" He shifted his weight from one foot to the other and back again.

"I don't know."

"If he doesn't, what happens to us?"

She couldn't look him in the eye but gazed at the leaves dancing in the wind. "You know I can't leave my home, my family or my church. This is where I belong. They have been so kind to me since Daniel died. They've helped me with Joseph. How can I walk away from this place where I belong?" She bit her lower lip. If he left, only little pieces of her would remain.

"Then I won't ask anything of you until I hear from Bishop Zook. But know this. I love you. I'll never stop loving you." He hopped in his buggy and clicked to his horse.

For the longest time after he left, she stood staring at the spot where he'd turned out of sight. "I love you, too, Elam Yoder."

Chapter Twenty-One

In the dimming daylight, Elam slid open the barn's big door, his muscles straining with the task. He stepped through the opening, the sweet smell of hay and the pungent odor of cow manure welcoming him. He'd missed this while he was gone. He moved to the back of the building where the truck sat covered with a tarp. He drew it back and examined his vehicle. The body shop did an expert job. Even though he knew where the damage had been, he couldn't tell the truck had ever been in such a terrible accident. No dents, no dings, no scrapes.

Before he sold it, he'd have to give it a thorough cleaning, inside and out. Maybe buy one of those pine-scented cardboard trees to hang from the rearview mirror to get rid of the farm stench. And then wash his hands of it forever.

He opened the door and retrieved the key from under the floor mat, the metal of it cool and smooth in his hand. When he'd driven it last, it had been fine, but he should probably at least change the oil and check the tire pressure before he put a for-sale sign on it.

After taking a deep breath, he slid into the driver's seat and turned the ignition. The truck roared to life. He pushed the gas pedal a few times. The engine hummed. Good. Maybe he wouldn't have to do any other maintenance to it.

Just as he was about to turn the truck off, Naomi entered the barn, Joseph in her arms. With the dying light behind her, she was beautiful. He couldn't breathe. She loved him. If only the bishop would see fit to restore him. Then they could be married. He forced in a lungful of air.

What he wanted most in the world stood just outside his grasp.

She came to the driver's side of the truck, and he cut the engine and slid out. "I'm surprised to see you here. What brought you by?"

She gave him a shy smile, the light reaching her eyes, almost violet to complement the color of her dress. "I was at the store for a few things Mamm needed, and I saw you go into the barn. You piqued my curiosity when you started the engine." Joseph wriggled and gasped for breath. "I don't know what drew me inside. You, possibly?"

His heart somersaulted. Was she flirting with him? "I'm glad you did." His words came out in a croaked whisper.

"Have you heard anything from Bishop Zook?"

"Not a word."

"This waiting is hard." She stepped closer, so close that Joseph reached out and grabbed his shirt.

Never had she been so beautiful, a tendril of chestnut hair escaping the bun at the base of her neck, curling around her collarbone. He leaned closer and gave her a gentle kiss, her lips soft, tasting of sugar. Better than he remembered.

What was he doing? He straightened and backed against the truck. "I'm sorry."

"I'm not."

His head swam. "You don't have anything to be sorry about, like I do. I shouldn't have started something we might not be able to finish. You can't leave, and I might not be able to stay. More than anything, I want to build a family with you. If the bishop won't baptize me, that won't be possible. I refuse to hurt you that way again." His chest ached.

She nodded. "Then we have to pray that the bishop will allow you to join the church. Because if you left, I would miss you very much. Maybe even more than before."

He groaned and rubbed his temples.

"I wish there was something I could do."

Joseph reached for Elam, and he took the *bobbeli* from his mother. Better for him to hold the baby. Then he wouldn't be able to take Naomi into his arms. "There is nothing to be done. All we can do is wait for the decision."

She glanced away, studying the length of the truck. "Were you going somewhere?"

"*Nein*, just making sure it still ran. I'm going to sell it. That's something I should have done long ago. When I first got back. It's a reminder of an awful time in my life. Our lives."

"But you did get me and Joseph to the clinic when he was so sick, so something *gut* came of it."

He blinked as he stared at her, her eyes wide in her heart-shaped face. This was a different Naomi. Not the sorrowing, frightened, closed-in woman of a few months ago.

"I never even thanked you for that."

"There was no need for you to. I was glad to help."

"You've been nothing but *gut* to us, and all I did was treat you badly. In fact, I have a surprise for you to make up for that. Simon and Sylvia have agreed to let you use their barn to start your business."

"You arranged that for me?"

She nodded. "To show you my appreciation for what you've done for us and to make up in a small way for the hurt I caused you. I shouldn't have shut you out the way I did. When you came to me after the accident, I should have listened to you. Maybe I could have spared you some pain. Perhaps things would have been different."

"*Denki.* I can't thank you enough. That you should do this for me." He swallowed hard. "I'll be able to start sooner than I dared to hope. What has changed you?"

"Aaron. Daniel. And God. Mostly God. Aaron shared a verse with me. About God blotting out our sins and remembering them no more. That is what true forgiveness is all about. When I realized that, I was able to let go of the past. Everything. The accident. You leaving. Daniel dying. I'm ready to embrace the future."

His throat constricted. "But that future might not include me."

Naomi bent over the green bean plants, the pods full and ripe. She snapped several off and dropped them in the basket beside her. She, Mamm and Laura had a great deal of work ahead of them, canning this haul of beans. But eating them cooked in bacon fat in February made all the hard work worth it.

She stood and worked a kink out of her back. Elam's words from yesterday rang in her head. If the bishop refused to baptize Elam, he wouldn't stay. And she wouldn't go. She couldn't. Everything she knew, everything she held dear, was here. Even with how much she loved him, she would never leave.

He had told her there was nothing they could do but pray. *Ja*, that was a *gut* thing to do, for sure and certain. Was it the only thing?

Maybe there was something else. Maybe there was a way she could influence the outcome. She brushed off her dirty hands, stepped over the ruts in the garden and went to the house.

Mamm didn't even glance up from her blackberry jam. "Done with those beans already?"

"I'll finish them later. I have an errand to

run right now. Can you watch Joseph for a while more?"

"Of course I can. You don't even need to ask. Where are you going?"

"It's sort of private. I'd rather not say. At least not right now."

At this, Mamm did turn to her. "What is going on? You've been different the past few days. Almost...well, almost glowing."

Naomi covered her mouth and shook her head. "It's your imagination."

"I think it has something to do with a certain young man."

She shrugged.

"Be careful."

She kissed Mamm's cheek. "I must get on with my errand. I'll see you later." She washed her hands and slipped off her dirty apron before harnessing the horse to the buggy. Coneflowers and daylilies bloomed along the side of the road, a riot of purple and orange.

She didn't have far to go to get to her destination. In short order, she pulled into Bishop Zook's driveway. She brought the horse to a halt. Martha, crouched over the beans in her own garden, stood and waved to her. "Come, come, tell me what's brought you by today."

Naomi scrambled across the garden, silk

drooping from the corn stalks, little green tomatoes clinging to the plants. "Your garden looks *wunderbaar* this year."

"The Lord blessed us with plenty of rain." Martha laughed. "I'm glad there wasn't much water toting needed this year."

"You're right."

"Let's go in the house, and I'll put on the coffeepot."

"I've actually come to speak to your husband."

"*Ach*, just like Elam a week or so ago. I think you'll find Reuben in the tack room. Come inside first, though, and take a thermos of coffee with you. No one should have a chat without at least a coffee cup in their hands."

That statement just about summed up Martha Zook. Since there was no point in arguing with her, Naomi got the thermos and two cups and went to find the bishop.

He was in the tack room, just as Martha said, oiling the reins and harnesses. She knocked on the door so she didn't scare him.

"Naomi, what a pleasant surprise. To what do I owe this visit?"

"I need to talk to you about something. But first, I've brought coffee from your wife. She said we couldn't talk without it."

Reuben chuckled, the melody like a deep

wind chime. "That sounds like my Martha. Have a seat and pour us each a cup."

Once they each held a steaming mug, the bishop leaned back, the old wooden office chair creaking, and crossed his legs. "What is it you want to talk to me about? I can almost guess why you're here."

"And you'd be right. Elam told me he stopped by not too long ago to confess and to request to be baptized. I've come to ask that you grant his request."

Chapter Twenty-Two

The Englischer popped the hood of Elam's truck and bent over the engine, examining the belts and checking the oil and transmission fluid levels. "Nice and clean. When was the last time you said you drove it?"

"A few weeks ago. But I just changed the oil, and it runs good." Elam held back the excitement in his voice. A potential buyer for his truck after only one day for sale.

The man flipped off his baseball cap and scratched his shaved head. "Has it ever been in an accident?"

Elam swallowed hard. "Yes." The word squeaked by his lips.

"How bad was the damage?"

"The front passenger side was pretty mangled. But the body shop did a full repair. It's as good as new."

"I'm going to have to think about it." The man meandered around the truck one more time.

Nein, Elam needed the man to buy the truck. Right here and now. Where had this urge to be rid of the vehicle as soon as possible come from? Like some force had hit him from behind and propelled him forward. "There isn't a scratch on it now."

"It is in good shape." The man chomped on a piece of gum. "But it sounds like it was a serious accident. What happened?"

Why had Elam pushed? Now he had to explain. He drew in a deep breath. "I hit a tree while I was on my cell phone."

"So why are you getting rid of it?"

Elam almost laughed at the absurdity of the question. "I'm joining the Amish church, and we're not allowed to have cars. That's the only reason." And he didn't mind giving up his truck. Not anymore. They were fast, dangerous and only got you into trouble. Much better to stick with a horse and buggy. People got hurt in those, certainly, but not like in cars.

The man stood facing the truck's grille, legs akimbo. "That accident makes me nervous."

"It wasn't the truck's fault." Elam grinned.

The man, Payton, chuckled. "I suppose not.

But a damaged frame is a concern. It makes the truck less safe in the case of another accident."

Elam nodded. He fidgeted with the hem of his jacket.

"Well, let me sleep on it. I'll be back if I decide to go with it." Payton turned toward the barn's entrance and took five steps in that direction.

"I'll take a thousand dollars off the price." The words slipped from Elam's mouth before he could check them.

Payton stopped and rubbed the back of his neck. "I don't know. You're tempting me."

Gut. In this case, temptation was a very *gut* thing.

"But I still want to think about it."

"Fifteen hundred dollars discount if you buy it today. That's my final offer." Elam hugged himself and held his breath.

Payton turned around. "Your final offer?"

What if he walked away? He wouldn't come back. Elam would lose this potential buyer. But maybe the man was testing him. "Yes. It's more than a fair price."

A slow smile spread across Payton's tanned face, and he stuck out his hand to shake Elam's. "You have yourself a deal. I'll run to the bank and be back with your money in about an hour."

Elam released his breath in a slow stream. "I'll have it ready to go for you then."

Payton was as good as his word. An hour later, Elam signed the title over to him, took the cash and stood at the end of the driveway as Payton drove the black pickup down the street, over the hill and out of sight.

He covered his face and breathed in and out. A knot that had kinked his stomach for a long time loosened. Like closing out the year on financial statements, he could shut the cover to this part of his life and start with a clean record book.

He fingered the money in his pocket. Even though he'd given Payton a hefty discount on the vehicle, Elam still possessed a wad of cash. Maybe he could buy Naomi something. But as a Plain woman, she didn't need anything. Perhaps it would go a fair way in a down payment on a house for them and Joseph. That was a *gut* idea, but not the right thing to do with the money.

Ja, there was one person this money belonged to. Elam strolled to the barn and hitched up the buggy. From now on, this would be his only means of transportation. He smiled and gave a one-note laugh at the way Naomi had held on to the truck's seat for dear life when he drove her to the clinic. She wouldn't have to do that in the buggy.

Because it was Friday, Naomi would be at the bakery, not at home, and that was a *gut* thing. Today he didn't pull into the Bontragers' driveway to see her. Instead, he parked near the wood shop and entered.

Naomi's daed pounded a dovetail joint together.

Elam stepped farther in, holding the envelope in his hand behind his back. "Hello."

Her daed peered up and harrumphed. "Thought I told you never to come back."

"Actually, I came to see Aaron. Is he around?"

Leroy nodded in the direction of the back room. "But don't bother him long. He has work to do."

"I won't." Elam followed the pungent stench of varnish to where he found Aaron staining a long dining room table. He whistled. "That's beautiful."

Aaron glanced up for a moment and grinned before returning his attention to his work. "*Denki.* I can see a large family gathering around it for special meals like Thanksgiving and Christmas." A wistfulness tainted his words.

"You do exceptional work. I take it you

haven't told your daed about our business venture yet."

Aaron concentrated on the job in front of him. "I haven't found the right time for the announcement."

"You can back out if you want. We don't have to go through with the deal."

"I will. Tell him, I mean."

"He told me not to keep you, so I won't." He handed the envelope to Aaron. "This is yours. It's not much, but I hope it helps you in some way."

Elam spun around and hurried through the room, the main shop and outside. He had almost made it to his buggy when Naomi crossed the street from the bakery. "Elam, I didn't expect you."

"I came to see—"

"Joseph has a doctor's appointment. Frank should be here any minute."

"Elam." The gravel crunched under the wheels of Aaron's chair.

Elam's heart pounded faster than a galloping horse.

Naomi glanced between Aaron and Elam. Elam's face resembled that of a fresh January snowfall. Aaron's was as red as a September sunset.

"Elam, wait." Aaron, breathless, motored across the yard. "I can't take this from you."

"*Nein*, I want you to have it." Elam stepped into his buggy.

Naomi went to him. "What's going on?"

"Nothing. This is between me and Aaron." He turned to her brother. "And don't say anything to her about it."

Naomi's windpipe closed, and she stomped her foot. "What are you talking about? Will someone please tell me?"

Aaron arrived at the buggy, sweat pouring from under his straw hat and down his face. In his hand, he held an envelope. "I don't know why you're giving this to me, but it belongs to you."

Naomi snatched the envelope from her brother. Elam reached out to grab it away, but she stepped back.

"Please, don't open it. This doesn't concern you."

She hesitated a moment. Elam widened his eyes and shook his head.

"Go ahead, Naomi." Aaron nudged her. "See what's in it."

She lifted the flap. Elam groaned. She gasped. "What is all this?"

"It's a lot of money. Money he gave me and told me was mine."

Naomi turned to Elam. "Is it his?"

"In a way, *ja*." Elam did little more than whisper. "It's my money, and I want him to have it. By rights, it belongs to him."

Naomi furrowed her brow. "Will one of you explain?"

Aaron shrugged. "It'll have to be him, because I don't understand myself. What do you mean that it belongs to me?"

"I sold my truck."

Naomi almost missed the soft-spoken words. Her mouth went dry. "You sold it?"

"Ja."

"It's gone."

Elam nodded. "And I can't say I'm sorry about it."

She couldn't stop the smile from stretching across her face. "Thank God. We can say goodbye to that chapter in our lives. Close the door and lock it. But what does this have to do with the money?"

"Those are the proceeds from the sale. Every penny the man paid me."

Aaron's mouth opened, but no words came out.

Naomi spoke for him. "Why?"

"It was me and my miserable truck that put him where he is today. Where he always will be."

Naomi drew in a breath to speak, but Elam raised his hand to stop her.

"Your family has gone through an awful time, in large part because of me. You have enough expenses with Joseph's care. I want to help. To ease your burden in whatever small way I can."

Naomi's knees buckled, and she leaned against Elam's buggy to stay upright. "You did that? For us?"

He touched her cheek, his fingertips cold against her warm skin. "No, *Liebchen*, I didn't do it for you, or for Aaron, or even for myself. I did it for God. He has given me so much. I have no right to keep the money. It was money that should never have been spent on an item I should never have bought. In the Englisch world, they call that coming full circle. It just means that everything is back to the beginning. To the way it should be. At least as much as it ever will be."

She couldn't stop the tears that tracked down her face and dripped from her chin. If only Aaron weren't looking, she would kiss Elam right then and there. Instead she grasped him by the hand. "You are a *gut* man, Elam Yoder. I am sorry I ever doubted you. *Ich liebe dich.* I love you." Was it possible for a heart to overflow with such emotion?

Aaron backed up his chair and headed toward the shop. "You two need some time alone." His chuckle faded as he went inside.

Elam kissed the palm of her hand. "This is why I didn't want you to find out. Because I knew you would get weepy."

"Is there anything wrong with that?"

"*Nein*, but I don't want you to get your hopes up. I still haven't heard from the bishop."

How could she ever live without this man in her life? She bit her lip. What was most important to her? "I—"

"Don't you ever, ever say it. Because I could never ask it of you."

"But you sold your truck. What happens if the bishop says no? And you gave your money to Aaron."

"I will have the business I'm starting, so I'll be fine. God will provide. He always does."

"But—"

"Please, don't say anything more. You have to get Joseph to the doctor, remember?"

She swiped the tears from her eyes just as Frank's white van pulled up the driveway. "I need to go." By the time she finished getting the words out of her mouth, Elam had already clucked to his horse and was on his way toward the street.

She stood as still as a deer in the woods that knows he's been spotted and stared as the orange caution triangle on the back of his buggy disappeared.

At the banging shut of Frank's van door, she jumped.

"Are you just about ready to leave? Where's that handsome son of yours?"

"I'll go get him." She turned to the house.

"Naomi, wait."

At Daed's voice, she spun around again. "I'm late for Joseph's appointment."

"I want to know what is going on between you and Elam."

She glanced in Frank's direction, and then back at Daed. "I can't go into it now. Can we talk later?"

"You can be sure we will."

Chapter Twenty-Three

In the glow of the gas lantern light, Naomi sat in the rocker in the living room, Joseph in her lap as she lulled him to sleep. Daed sat across from her in his big recliner, the family's German Luther Bible in his hands, Mamm and Laura on the couch, Aaron in his chair in the corner, near the wood-burning stove. Would they still gather like this when she moved next door? These nights would be a thing of the past if she married Elam.

If. The question hung over her head.

Daed leafed through the pages, searching for a passage to read for family devotions. He found the spot where they left off last night, and intoned the words of Scripture. Naomi rocked to the cadence of his speech.

What if she lost Elam? Could she stand the hole he would leave in her heart? Once he had been ripped from her. A second time might leave a wound from which she would never recover.

She scanned the room. Laura fidgeted with the hem of her apron and tapped her foot. Always on the go, she had a hard time sitting still every evening for the Bible reading. Sunday services were pure torture for her. The same for Samuel, who wriggled more than Joseph.

Beside her, Mamm sat with her hands folded on her lap, gazing at her husband, never wavering. Solid and steady, that was Mamm.

And Aaron, sitting straight in his chair, focused on the darkness outside the window, wise beyond his years. Was he as truly happy and content as he led the world to believe?

If the decision came down to Elam or her family, could she choose? If she could but split herself in half and be both places at once.

Daed coughed. He had finished the reading. The rest of her family bowed their heads in silent prayer. She followed suit. *God, please soften the bishop's heart. Allow us to be together here, in this place I love the most. I can't make this decision myself. Don't let me have to make it.*

The family stirred, and she opened her eyes. Daed rose to get ready for bed.

Aaron fidgeted and then spoke. "Can everyone stay for just a minute more? I have something to announce." His eyes didn't twinkle, and no smile lifted the corners of his mouth. He rubbed the arms of his wheelchair. What was coming?

Daed returned to his chair, and Mamm settled on the couch again. Laura shook her head. "Will this take long?"

"As you know, Elam came to see me this afternoon."

"Is that all this is about?" Laura stood.

Mamm pulled her down. "Listen to your brother without interruption."

"*Ja*, that is what this is about. He told me he sold his truck, the one involved in the... accident. And he handed me an envelope. In it was all the money from the sale of his vehicle. Thousands of dollars."

Mamm gasped. Even Daed sat forward. "Why would he do such a foolish thing?"

"It's not foolish. He wants to help our family. He knows we have more than our share of doctor expenses. Even though the auction brought in plenty, this will keep us from dipping into the medical fund and leave more for others. That's the kind of man Elam Yoder is."

Daed frowned.

"And there's one more thing. In a few weeks, I'm going into business with him. He's starting a firm that makes outdoor furniture, and I want to be part of it. He has agreed to make me a partner."

"I will not have you leaving the family business to take on a venture with that man." Daed raised his shoulders and puffed out his chest. "Who will work with me?"

"You have Solomon. And in a few years, you'll have Samuel. They are more capable than I am."

"But I need you."

"You don't. With the little I do, you won't notice I'm gone. I'd like to try a different job, one that utilizes more of my skills."

Daed grunted, his eyes narrow.

Naomi jumped to her feet, startling Joseph awake. She shushed him, and he closed his eyes again. "Before you say anything, Daed, I agree with Aaron and think you should allow them to work together. Elam made a mistake. That was almost four years ago already."

"A mistake that was as much my fault as his. I told him to call ahead for pizza. If I hadn't done that…"

Daed slapped his thigh. "I will not have you blaming yourself for what happened."

Naomi stared at Daed. "Then you shouldn't

blame Elam either. It's time to we moved past this. Isn't that the way of our people?"

"*Ja*, but—"

"No more *buts*. Remember the story from years ago about the shooting at the West Nickel Mines School in Pennsylvania? Families had children, little girls, who were gunned down there in cold blood. But that very night, in the midst of their grief, they visited the shooter's family, to offer them comfort in their loss."

"I recall that. You don't have to remind me." But a bit of the gruffness left Daed's voice.

Naomi, still clutching Joseph to her, kneeled in front of Daed. "Then how can we do any less? We still have Aaron with us. If they could see past their own tragedy to others' pain the same night it happened, shouldn't we be able to do that after so much time? And I happen to know that Elam went…" She bit her tongue. Maybe he didn't want the world to know.

Daed cupped her chin. "What has he done?"

She lowered her gaze.

"Tell me."

"He went to Bishop Zook and confessed all his wrongs. Everything. The accident. The papers. He's asked to be baptized, but the bishop is still making up his mind, weighing whether or not Elam's confession is sincere. And I went to see the bishop myself."

Daed drew his brows together. "Why would you do such a thing?"

"Because I love Elam, and I know he's changed. He's not the same person who left here in disgrace. In the time he was away, Elam grew up. Gone is the rash young man he used to be. He's wise, thoughtful and the most caring man I've ever met. His confession is a true repentance. That's what I told the bishop, and I asked him to accept Elam and baptize him."

"You love him?"

Naomi turned toward Mamm, who wiped a tear from her eye. "*Ja*, I do, very much. I haven't come to this conclusion quickly or easily. But once I let go of the past and truly forgave Elam, the bitterness and the grief disappeared and left only love for him."

Aaron leaned forward. "It's past time for us and everyone around here to embrace him into the fold. If God can forgive us, can't we do the same with Elam?"

Naomi turned back to Daed. "Can't you find it in your heart?"

Daed gave the smallest of nods. "Convicted by my children. *Ja*, you are right. It is time to count our blessings and not dwell on the things of the past."

Now, if only the bishop would make up his mind.

Never before had the sight of Elam's green-roofed white farmhouse looked so *gut* to him. Not even the day he'd come home after being gone for so long.

With the height of the summer upon them, the construction boss worked the crew extra hard. They had enough orders to keep them more than busy until the snow flew. And then there were the details to put together to start the new business in August. Elam yawned and stretched as Vern pulled into the driveway. If he could get a decent night's sleep, that would help. But all day and all night, he tossed and turned. What if the bishop refused to baptize him? What if he lost Naomi for a second time? He wouldn't be able to bear it. He'd be forced to leave this place and start over where he would forget about her.

As if he ever could.

He'd tried that once. And failed.

He'd done all that was possible. Now it was time to leave his future in the Lord's hands. A hard thing to do.

A buggy sat near the barn, and not one that

belonged to any of his family members. Perhaps a friend of Mamm's had come to visit her.

Elam slipped from the van. "Thanks, Vern. I'll see you tomorrow."

Vern waved as he backed down the drive. As Elam climbed the steps to the porch, his stomach twisted. His lunch must not have agreed with him.

Mamm greeted him at the door. "I'm glad you're home. You look exhausted. But never mind that. You have a visitor. He's with Daed in the living room. Wash up and go see him."

"Aren't you going to give me a clue?" Elam worked to smile.

She shook her head, though a light shone in her green eyes. "Come and get the dirt off yourself."

Like he was a little boy again, he went to the sink in obedience to his mamm. He splashed cold water on his face. That woke him up. After drying his hands on a towel, he meandered to the living room, taking his time, his middle clenching and unclenching. Daed sat in his favorite, well-worn brown chair next to the window.

On the plain blue couch sat Bishop Zook.

Elam's lungs shut down and dizziness scrambled his head. "Bishop, it's *gut* to see you." Enough small talk. They both knew why the bishop had paid a call. "I assume you made your decision about my baptism."

"Have a seat, Elam."

This couldn't be good. If the bishop had accepted his confession, he would have come right out and said so. He wouldn't stall. Elam sat and clasped his hands together to keep them from trembling.

The bishop crossed his legs. "I appreciate your coming to see me and repenting of your sins. You have a tendency to be rash, but I hope you have learned your lesson."

"I have. From now on, I will think through each of my decisions very carefully, and weigh every possible outcome before I act."

"Naomi visited me several days ago."

"She did?" Why?

"*Ja.* You are a blessed young man to have a woman such as her to love you."

Heat crept up Elam's neck. "That's for sure and certain."

"And such a wise woman at that. She spoke well of you and had such a humble and compassionate heart. She made me stop and take a good look at myself and how I was thinking about forgiveness. And about how I was treating you."

Had she overstepped her bounds with the

bishop? Gone too far? Not that he would ever blame her for trying. He loved her all the more for it.

"Given everything I've heard from both you and Naomi and from talks I've had with Aaron, the elders and I have come to the conclusion…"

Blood pounded in Elam's ears.

"…that your confession was sincere. We agree to baptize you and welcome you to our church, if you are still sure that is what you want."

Had he heard that correctly? "You're accepting me back?"

The bishop nodded. "*Ja*, I am."

The one good corner of Daed's mouth turned up into a grin. "I'm happy for you, son."

Mamm, who must have been in the room the entire time, came to him and enveloped him in a hug. "Thank God, you are truly home for *gut*. No more wandering for you."

A surge of energy rushed through him, like the time he'd shocked himself on a frayed drill cord. "*Denki*, bishop, *denki*. I cannot thank you enough. We will set the date very soon. As soon as possible. But right now, I have to go somewhere. Please excuse me."

He raced from the house. As fast as his

shaking hands allowed him, he harnessed the buggy horse and set off. He urged Prancer down the street at a rapid pace. All the way, he rehearsed what he would say and how he would say it once he arrived at his destination.

Chapter Twenty-Four

Naomi stood at the kitchen sink washing dishes, up to her elbows in suds, when a buggy raced up the driveway. She shivered. Something must be wrong for whoever drove to be so wild. Hadn't they had their share of problems and trials? Couldn't they have a period of peace and rest?

Behind her, Joseph, who had been playing on the floor, cried. She grabbed a dish towel and dried her arms then picked up her son. She kissed his round cheeks and his high forehead. "What's wrong, my *bobbeli*? Don't worry. Whatever has happened, Mamm will keep you safe." His surgery still lay in front of him. She squeezed him, and he protested louder. "*Ach*, I'm sorry."

A rapid pounding sounded on the door. Mamm and Daed read *The Budget* in the living room, and the others, well, who knew where they'd gone to. Jiggling Joseph on her hip, she went to the door, trembling as she turned the knob.

And then she stumbled backward against the wall. "Elam." She clutched her chest. Something terrible must have happened for him to fly up the driveway at breakneck speed. "What's wrong?"

He grinned. Grinned? "Nothing is wrong, *Liebchen*, absolutely nothing." Light danced in his eyes. "Get your sweater. We're going to take a walk."

"Don't scare me like that. With the way you worked that horse, I thought we had another tragedy on our hands. All that for a walk? But why?"

"Grab a blanket for Joseph, too. He should come with us, I think."

"Again, why?"

His smile vanished, and he stared at her, his eyes hard, though his features remained soft. She squirmed.

"Don't you trust me?" His voice was a breathy whisper.

"Of course I do."

"Then let's get going."

"The dishes need to be finished."

"I'll help you when we get back."

"But—"

"Naomi, please."

His behavior was out of character, even for him. What was going on? She shrugged and sighed. "Fine." While she pulled on her sweater, Elam wrapped Joseph in a fleecy blue blanket. The summer evening held an uncharacteristic chill.

This was crazy.

Naomi popped into the living room, and Mamm glanced up from her reading. "Elam is here. We're going for a quick walk and taking Joseph. We won't be gone long. I'll finish the dishes when I get back."

"Have a *gut* time."

Daed glanced up, his lips pinched. To his credit, he didn't forbid her to go.

They set off from the house along the lane that led to the fields and the woods behind. Elam walked so fast she had to almost run to keep up with him. "Slow down. What is your hurry?"

He halted, color rising in his cheeks. "I'm sorry. I forget sometimes that my legs are so much longer than yours." He pointed to the trees ahead of them. "Look at how the setting sun is brushing them with fire. Now I know why the Amish don't have many pictures and such in their homes. Look at the beauty God gave all around us. That is what He wants us to appreciate."

"That's a fancy way of saying the leaves are pretty."

He chuckled, low and steady, like rolling thunder. "You are right." He clasped her chilly hand in his warm one, and they walked on for a while.

"So why did you really bring me here?" Joseph bounced in her arms and clapped his hands.

"He has a new trick I see."

"*Ja*, he claps all the time now. But in a short bit, he's going to start fussing. It's almost his bedtime."

They wandered down the path toward the little stream. This time of year, it still babbled over the rocks. Not for much longer. When midsummer's dry spell inevitably arrived, it halted the brook's gurgling.

Once they reached the water, he sat on the trunk of a downed tree and pulled her beside him. Was he shaking? Maybe something really was wrong.

"You are the most beautiful, the sweetest, the most remarkable woman I have ever met in my life. Do you remember the last time I brought you to this spot?"

She glanced around at the trees, their green

leaves forming a canopy over them. *Ja*, this place held a certain familiarity. When she'd been young, she had come here all the time and splashed in the water and made mud pies. Mamm would scold her when she came home with dirt streaked down her apron, the hem of her dress wet.

And when they'd been courting, Elam brought her here often, stealing a kiss or two from her. But the last time…

She sucked in her breath. Tears clogged her throat. "The last time you brought me here was when you proposed."

He nodded, stared at her and licked his lips. "When I came home from work today, a visitor waited for me."

She raised her eyebrows as Joseph tugged on her prayer *kapp* strings. Her heart hammered.

"The bishop."

Her hands sweated. "Has he made his decision?"

"Ja."

She turned from Elam, unable to bear the pain in his eyes when he told her the bishop refused to baptize him. "And?" The word came out on a puff of air.

"I'm to be baptized as soon as possible."

Elam's breath on her neck sent shivers

down her spine. She spun to face him. "He did? Oh, really?"

"Ja, ja." That silly grin spread across his face again. The grin she loved more than anything in the world.

"That's *wunderbaar* news. The best ever."

He slid close to her and pulled her against his chest. *"Ich liebe dich*, Naomi. I love you more than ever. More than when we were here the last time. I brought you here for a special reason. Because I want to ask you an important question."

Joseph snuggled against her. "What is that?" Was this really happening a second time?

"Will you marry me? I promise to love you and Joseph and always take care of you and him and—"

With a soft kiss on his lips, she shushed him. *"Ja*, Elam Yoder, nothing would make me happier than to be your wife."

Joseph gurgled and sighed. Elam laughed. "I would say he approves of the arrangement." His voice caught. "I'm so proud that I'll be his daed."

"He can't be any happier than I am at the moment." If God blessed her any more, her heart would burst.

Epilogue

"Happy birthday, my sweet *bobbeli*." Naomi pulled Joseph from where he stood in his crib, kissed his plump cheek and set him on the floor. On his hands and knees, he rocked back and forth.

Without warning, Elam snuck up behind her and encircled her waist. "You won't be able to call him a *bobbeli* much longer. Look how big he's getting."

She turned in her husband's arms and kissed him. Oh, what a surprise awaited him if her suspicions were correct. By Joseph's second birthday, he would be a big brother. But today was Joseph's day. A time to celebrate his life and his health, how he endured the surgery and was now a robust little boy. "He's going to love the little chair you made for him."

"I hope so. That can be another line for my shop. Outdoor furniture for children."

"What a *wunderbaar* idea. Already God is blessing your business. Joseph is going to be thrilled with the train Aaron is giving him, even though he isn't walking yet to pull it around. And I can't wait for his reaction to the cake I'm making."

"I think you're more excited about the party than Joseph." He chuckled, rich and full and deep.

Just like their life now. She touched his bearded cheek. "How could I have ever doubted that you're the man God intended for me? I can't imagine my life without you."

He bent over and kissed her, pulling her close, squeezing her until she ran out of breath and had to pull away. She swatted his bicep. "What will my parents think if they come over and find us like this?"

"They'll think we're a very happy newly-wed couple, that's what."

He smooched with her once more before she slipped from his embrace, laughing. "I have to get dinner ready before our families arrive. And since Joseph now has three sets of grandparents, it's going to have to be a big meal."

"Your fault for marrying me." He tugged

on her prayer *kapp* string and kissed her on the cheek.

On the floor at their feet, Joseph gurgled, but she gazed at her husband. How could one woman be so blessed?

Elam grabbed her by the shoulder and shook her. "Look at Joseph. Watch him go."

Sure enough, there went Joseph crawling across his bedroom floor toward the door. She couldn't squelch the squeal that burst inside her. "He's crawling. See that? He's doing it." At the room's threshold, she scooped him up and bear-hugged him. "You're such a big boy."

"Don't leave me out." Elam wrapped both of them in an embrace.

For a moment, Naomi closed her eyes. *Denki, Lord, for this family.* When she opened her eyes, she drank in the sight of her husband and her son. "Come on, you two. Time to celebrate."

* * * * *

*If you loved this story,
be sure to pick up these other
amazing Amish titles.*

AN UNEXPECTED AMISH ROMANCE
by Patricia Davids
AN AMISH ARRANGEMENT
by Jo Ann Brown
A MAN FOR HONOR *by Emma Miller*

Available now from Love Inspired!

*Find more great reads at
www.LoveInspired.com*

Dear Reader,

Thank you for joining me for Naomi and Elam's journey. About seven or eight years ago, I discovered that Wisconsin has several large and thriving Amish communities. In fact, it boasts the fourth-largest Amish population in the country. Who knew? I've enjoyed getting to know more about the people and what their lives are like.

One day, as I was in line at the bakery (because who can resist a still-warm doughnut or a pretzel as big as your head), I spied a young Amish girl by the barn. She gave me a shy smile, and I discovered that she had Down syndrome. As the mother of a special needs child myself, I wondered how the Amish deal with those with disabilities. And so the idea for this book sprouted.

While this is a story of loss and heartache, it's also a story of forgiveness and triumph. The Lord has forgiven us of so much, and because of this, we are free to forgive others and forget about the past. My prayer is that you will be blessed by reading this book.

All the best,

Liz

Get 4 FREE REWARDS!

We'll send you 2 FREE Books plus 2 FREE Mystery Gifts.

Love Inspired® Suspense books feature Christian characters facing challenges to their faith... and lives.

FREE Value Over $20

YES! Please send me 2 FREE Love Inspired® Suspense novels and my 2 FREE mystery gifts (gifts are worth about $10 retail). After receiving them, if I don't wish to receive any more books, I can return the shipping statement marked "cancel." If I don't cancel, I will receive 4 brand-new novels every month and be billed just $5.24 each for the regular-print edition or $5.74 each for the larger-print edition in the U.S., or $5.74 each for the regular-print edition or $6.24 each for the larger-print edition in Canada. That's a savings of at least 13% off the cover price. It's quite a bargain! Shipping and handling is just 50¢ per book in the U.S. and 75¢ per book in Canada*. I understand that accepting the 2 free books and gifts places me under no obligation to buy anything. I can always return a shipment and cancel at any time. The free books and gifts are mine to keep no matter what I decide.

Choose one: ☐ **Love Inspired® Suspense**
Regular-Print
(153/353 IDN GMY5)

☐ **Love Inspired® Suspense**
Larger-Print
(107/307 IDN GMY5)

Name (please print)

Address   Apt. #

City   State/Province   Zip/Postal Code

Mail to the **Reader Service:**
IN U.S.A.: P.O. Box 1341, Buffalo, NY 14240-8531
IN CANADA: P.O. Box 603, Fort Erie, Ontario L2A 5X3

Want to try two free books from another series! Call 1-800-873-8635 or visit www.ReaderService.com.

---

*Terms and prices subject to change without notice. Prices do not include applicable taxes. Sales tax applicable in N.Y. Canadian residents will be charged applicable taxes. Offer not valid in Quebec. This offer is limited to one order per household. Books received may not be as shown. Not valid for current subscribers to Love Inspired Suspense books. All orders subject to approval. Credit or debit balances in a customer's account(s) may be offset by any other outstanding balance owed by or to the customer. Please allow 4 to 6 weeks for delivery. Offer available while quantities last.

Your Privacy—The Reader Service is committed to protecting your privacy. Our Privacy Policy is available online at www.ReaderService.com or upon request from the Reader Service. We make a portion of our mailing list available to reputable third parties that offer products we believe may interest you. If you prefer that we not exchange your name with third parties, or if you wish to clarify or modify your communication preferences, please visit us at www.ReaderService.com/consumerchoice or write to us at Reader Service Preference Service, P.O. Box 9062, Buffalo, NY 14240-9062. Include your complete name and address.

LIS18

Get 4 FREE REWARDS!

We'll send you 2 FREE Books plus 2 FREE Mystery Gifts.

Bad Boy Rancher
Karen Rock

Love Songs and Lullabies
Amy Vastine

Harlequin® Heartwarming™ Larger-Print books feature traditional values of home, family, community and most of all—love.

FREE
Value Over
$20

HOME on the RANCH

YES! Please send me the **Home on the Ranch Collection** in Larger Print. This collection begins with 3 FREE books and 2 FREE gifts in the first shipment. Along with my 3 free books, I'll also get the next 4 books from the Home on the Ranch Collection, in LARGER PRINT, which I may either return and owe nothing, or keep for the low price of $5.24 U.S./ $5.89 CDN each plus $2.99 for shipping and handling per shipment*. If I decide to continue, about once a month for 8 months I will get 6 or 7 more books, but will only need to pay for 4. That means 2 or 3 books in every shipment will be FREE! If I decide to keep the entire collection, I'll have paid for only 32 books because 19 books are FREE! I understand that accepting the 3 free books and gifts places me under no obligation to buy anything. I can always return a shipment and cancel at any time. My free books and gifts are mine to keep no matter what I decide.

268 HCN 3760 468 HCN 3760

Name	(PLEASE PRINT)

Address	Apt. #

City	State/Prov.	Zip/Postal Code

Signature (if under 18, a parent or guardian must sign)

Mail to the **Reader Service:**

IN U.S.A.: P.O. Box 1867, Buffalo, NY. 14240-1867
IN CANADA: P.O. Box 609, Fort Erie, Ontario L2A 5X3

* Terms and prices subject to change without notice. Prices do not include applicable taxes. Sales tax applicable in NY. Canadian residents will be charged applicable taxes. This offer is limited to one order per household. All orders subject to approval. Credit or debit balances in a customer's account(s) may be offset by any other outstanding balance owed by or to the customer. Please allow 3 to 4 weeks for delivery. Offer available while quantities last. Offer not available to Quebec residents.

HRCBPA18

READERSERVICE.COM

Manage your account online!
- Review your order history
- Manage your payments
- Update your address

We've designed the Reader Service website just for you.

Enjoy all the features!
- Discover new series available to you, and read excerpts from any series.
- Respond to mailings and special monthly offers.
- Browse the Bonus Bucks catalog and online-only exculsives.
- Share your feedback.

Visit us at:

ReaderService.com

RS16R